MICHELLE M. PILLOW

CAPTURED BY A DRAGON-SHIFTER

STRANDED
WITH THE CAJUN

A DRAGON LORDS ROMANCE

Captured by a Dragon-Shifter: Stranded with the Cajun

Stranded with the Cajun © copyright 2015 by Michelle M. Pillow
First Print Edition Publication Oct 2015
First Electronic Printing Jan 2016
Cover art by Ravven, © Copyright 2015

ISBN-13: 978-1517499419
ISBN-10: 1517499410

STRANDED
WITH THE CAJUN

A DRAGON LORDS ROMANCE

CAPTURED BY A DRAGON-SHIFTER

Determined Prince
Rebellious Prince
Mischievous Prince
Headstrong Prince

Stranded with a Cajun
More to Come!

NOTE FROM AUTHOR

If you're new to my books, the *Dragon Lords* are my bestselling futuristic romance series. The stories became reader favorites, and so I wrote things from their enemy's point of view in a spin-off series for the cat-shifting *Lords of the Var*. Then they ventured off into the stars in the series installment *Space Lords*. Now, I'm time traveling with them back to our time with the series *Captured by a Dragon-Shifter*, which you are now reading book one of. Don't worry, I have the series reading order on my website to help you figure it all out, www.michellepillow.com.

To those of you not new to my books, readers have emailed asking Dragon Lords cultural questions since the first dragon-shifting prince released years ago. I have teased you with a lot of little hints of how the Draig found brides in "the old days". Many of you have expressed wanting to climb aboard the space ship and sail away into the future—which would probably take some cryogenic freezing and a lot of icy waiting. Well, before you start packing those sweaters… I don't want any of you going to that extreme, so I've brought your favorite dragon-shifters and cat-shifters to modern-day Earth. They don't live on our planet, but they have recently started to revisit.

For *Dragon Lords* and *Lords of the Var* fans, *Captured by a Dragon-Shifter* is a modern-day prequel series to those first books. They take place long before the princes you know and love ever found their mates, long before *The Dragon's Queen*, in a time when the dragon-shifters and cat-shifters actually — wait for it — *liked* each other and hung out as friends. They also don't have Galaxy Brides to bring them women. There's no one left to marry on the planet and things are starting to get desperate.

Author recommends reading series installments in order of release for the simple fact she likes hiding little tidbits in the books as she goes and it's more fun that way, though each book can be read as a standalone if you prefer.

DEDICATION

To the dreamers and star gazers.

PROLOGUE

Two years ago...

Once a decision was made, it needed to remain made.

Dimosthenis had given this decision a lot of consideration. With his brother's death, he was the only remaining son to carry on the family bloodline. Unfortunately, to do that, he needed to leave everything behind and travel to Earth.

A mate wasn't easy to find on his planet of Qurilixen. He loved his home, the shadowed marshes where he grew up, the trees near the borderlands so thick they could have been walls, the mountains where he now stood on the precipice of his future. However, for as beautiful as it was, there was something darker beneath the surface, a curse.

The Draig people were dying. Not with disease or war, but because their population lacked females. With no women, there were no babies. He was part of an entire generation of dragon-shifter men who had no wives. Well, all but one — a prince. The royal family had opened the portal to Earth in order to find wives for themselves. They guarded it jealously and did not let commoners go through. He was sure they had their reasons, reasons that made sense to the rulers, but for the everyday man who spent lonely night after night without the comfort of a wife, it was particularly cruel. Dimosthenis deserved a chance to have a family, a wife, love.

He deserved a trip through the portal.

The porous black rocks of the cave held his future. He'd followed the human Princess Eve and her escort down the hidden stairwell from inside the palace, careful to stay out of sight, and now hid by the cave's exterior exit for his chance to go in. All he had to do was step inside the darkness. He may never get another opportunity. There were those shifter factions who wanted to seal the portals forever, who didn't think human women were the answer. They had plans to detonate the hidden chamber.

If he left, he could never come home.

If he stayed, he might never find a mate.

A soft purple glow lit the cave. They must have activated the portal. He crept forward to watch from the shadows. Dragons and cats were carved into the stone chamber, pointing away from the portal, a symbol of their exodus from Earth. The elders told campfire stories of the portal's magic, of how it brought them from Earth, away from the persecution of human warlords. Had the humans changed? Or were the horror stories of hunting and slaughtering dragons still an Earth reality? Surely not every dragon and cat-shifter on Earth came through the portal, many yes, but there was no way of knowing how many chose to stay behind.

Fear filled him. There was no guarantee that love awaited him on the other side of the portal. In fact, it might only be death. Earth could be an ugly place. It could be filled with dragon-hating hunters. It could bring him nothing but loneliness and pain. Perhaps there was a reason the royals did not invite commoners through. Maybe he should listen to what the elders said, to the will of the gods as translated for him, and go home to wait for a blessing that may never come.

No. He had to try. He had left goodbye messages for his friends. The decision he made in this moment determined the rest of his life. To stay meant being alone forever, which was as good as deciding to die today. So there was no choice. He would jump into the unknown.

CHAPTER ONE

Modern-Day Earth…

"Come on, Big Daddy, come on." Lori Johnston hit the man's stiff arm frantically. "I need you, Big Daddy."

She took several breaths before lifting her camera to use the flash to illuminate the dusk settling over the surrounding area. She hit the shutter release several times, snapping pictures. When she looked at the digital display, a swamp full of glowing eyes stared at her, reflecting the harsh light. Scary eyes. Hungry eyes. Prehistoric alligator eyes. She turned her small penlight over the stagnant water and muddy shoreline, hoping it would reveal something the camera had not.

Help was not hiding in the Spanish moss.

Her hands shook violently, causing the beam of light to dance. The creatures were out there, beyond the airboat, floating like eerie logs in the swamp, just waiting for the right moment to lunge and eat them.

"Please. I don't know what to do. I can't be stranded in the swamp. I just can't. I'm not made for this. Wake up, Big Daddy, why did you have to die on me?" Lori eyed the dead body on the flat bottom of the boat. Surely, someone would come looking for them? They'd been gone for hours. When they'd left the dock, everyone had waved to Big Daddy from the shoreline. Everyone. He was popular. People liked him. And why not? He looked like the Cajun version of Santa Claus and was probably just as old. They'd come looking for him when he didn't make it home. Unless they assumed the swamp life was so ingrained in him that he didn't need help right away.

Oh God. What if people thought she killed him? Or they blamed her? She was pretty sure horror movies were made about city slickers who became lost amongst the swamp folk. And if there weren't such movies, there should be because she was scared as hell right now.

Who knew what they'd think when she told them Big Daddy had hit the accelerator and yelled, "Whoo doggie!" before slumping over in his airboat captain's chair. She had screamed as the boat bounced. Maybe her scream had done it? No, no, that was ridiculous. Her scream hadn't given him a heart attack. Big Daddy was old. They knew he was old. She was giving in to unrealistic fears when she should be focusing on the hungry problems right in front of her.

Michelle M. Pillow

The airboat had run aground on a mud bank. She knew this because her shoe was also stuck in the mud. When she'd tried going for help, she'd sunk knee deep into the muck. The illusion of shore was a trap—a muddy, muddy quicksand of a trap. Even if she did make it to shore, she had no idea which way to go.

Lori slapped a mosquito on her neck. If the alligators didn't eat her first, the giant bugs would.

She shone the penlight over the water and counted the eyes. "One, two, three, four, six, eight…"

Was it her imagination, or were the alligators multiplying exponentially in number?

If her situation weren't so dire, it would be laughable. In the age of satellites and cell phones, she was in the middle of a swamp with no hope of salvation. She'd left her cell phone behind at the inn she was staying at. There was a device in her camera bag that synced her cell phone service to her camera so she could use GPS tracking while on shoots, but there was no way to make a call. For some reason, she'd thought disconnecting from the technical world today would be a great idea.

"Unplug. Unwind. Great idea," she whispered sarcastically. "Connect with nature by dying on an airboat in the middle of the swamp and spend eternity as alligator poop. Circle of life."

She'd paid for a dusk bayou tour hoping to get a few sunset photos for her travel article, so the last threads of daylight were fast fading into darkness. A loud splash sounded, and she turned her light toward the bald cypress trees growing out of the water. She held her breath, listening for movement. Another splash sounded. "Hello? Is someone there?"

Maybe it was the swamp monster the inn manager had joked about. The Bayou Lizard Man she'd called him. Apparently, there had been recent sightings. He was going to receive an honorable mention in Lori's article as a glimpse of local color.

More splashes sounded. She moved her tiny beam of light over the water. The eyes were disappearing. Water rippled where the alligators submerged. Lori climbed onto the driver's seat and pulled her knees against her chest. She turned the penlight off, worried that it might run out of batteries when she really needed it. Moonlight gave very little relief to the tree-cast shadows.

Humidity was high, causing her shirt to stick to her skin. The late summer heat was made all the more oppressive by the lack of a breeze. It sapped her energy and made it hard to concentrate. The bottle of warm water was half empty but, without knowing how long she'd be out there, she had to ration it.

Lori closed her eyes and hugged the penlight and camera to her chest. All she had to do was wait a few hours until dawn.

Suddenly, the boat shifted. A figured moved in the shadows near Big Daddy. Lori bit back her scream as she reached for her camera to rapid fire her flash. The strobe-like beam illuminated the end of the boat. She expected to see an alligator pulling the body into the water. Instead, she found a man crouching over Big Daddy's corpse. She fumbled for the penlight and dropped her camera. She shone the small beam in the man's direction.

The relief was short lived as the man turned his attention toward her. Yellow, reptilian eyes found hers. Dark brown skin glistened with moisture as if he'd just slithered up from the water. Taloned fingers touched Big Daddy's face.

"Li-li-li-li..." she whispered.

"What happened?" His hoarse voice jolted her to her senses. The light trembled, but she got the impression of fangs in his mouth.

"Li-li-lizard man," she said. "Lizard alligator man. Alli-alli-alli..."

"You are learning to speak?" The alligator man stood as if to come to her. All she saw was talons and fangs.

Lori didn't think. She jumped off the boat into the mud, holding the penlight tightly. Her feet instantly sank. A hissing noise made her more frantic to get away, but the more she struggled, the more the mud pulled her down.

"Cursed female, what..." The reptile man's harsh words were lost as he leaped after her.

A rumbling growl came from the other direction. She was trapped. A prehistoric head snapped at her. Lori tried to cover her face in defense when the alligator lunged at her.

The reptile man slid forward over the mud, jamming his arm right into the alligator's mouth. They struggled, alligator man and the beast, rolling over the moist earth in a fierce battle before falling into the water. Lori used every ounce of strength to pull herself back toward the boat. The mud claimed her last shoe and weighed down the cotton material of her skirt, making it hard to maneuver. Without thinking, she dropped the penlight over the boat's edge, pushed the skirt off her waist and left it behind as she crawled out of the mud into the boat.

Lori scrambled to pick up the penlight. In her haste, she moved too quickly and hit her head on the metal frame. She held her temple. A splash sounded in the water, and she swung around to see what was happening. Her judgment was off in the dark, and she smacked face-first into the airboat chair.

CHAPTER TWO

Drake didn't enjoy injuring the animal as he slammed his fist against the creature's scaly head, but it was the only way he knew to force it to let go of his arm. The pressure of the powerful jaws on his forearm hurt but the armor of his shifted skin protected him from severe injury. The alligator loosened his hold and Drake ripped his arm free so that he could surface for air.

Gasping for breath, he kicked in the alligator's direction a few times. The creature swam from him, and Drake was able to make his way onto the airboat. He grunted as he pulled himself out of the water.

The glow of the penlight illuminated the bottom of the boat, but he didn't need it. His shifted eyes cut through the darkness with ease. He reached for the unconscious woman lying next to the corpse of the old man. Her skin was warm, and he could see the rise and fall of her back as she breathed.

Stupid human.

What was she thinking by jumping into an alligator's mouth? Drake had only come through the portal to Earth a few years ago, and even he knew you didn't offer yourself up as a tasty snack to monsters with big teeth.

Not waiting around to see if another alligator would be attracted to the noise the underwater skirmish had made and come looking for a meal, Drake let his body shift into his human form and instantly set to work trying to get the boat to run.

Stupid dragon-shifter.

He shouldn't have scared her like that. What had he expected jumping up onto a boat in his shifted form? Those who knew his secret had warned him about showing others. But it wasn't as if he could swim the swamps at night without protection. The woman clearly needed help. And if Lady Big Daddy's poor decision-making skills in a crisis were any indication, she wasn't a local.

Wait. Miss. Here they called them miss, not my lady. Miss Big Daddy. Or was Big Daddy her father? Yes. That made the most sense.

The rudder stick was jammed and took some maneuvering, but he was able to get the airboat working again. Thankfully, the mud bank wasn't too high. He dislodged the bottom of the boat and returned it to the water.

The penlight bounced as he steered the boat through the dark swamps. Light danced over the unconscious woman's body. Her legs were bare and streaked with mud. Drake found himself studying her breathing more than watching where he drove. Something about her caused a strange feeling inside his chest like they had met before, and he kept waiting for recognition to come to him. A few times, he steered too close to the trees. Once, a small limb hit the fan behind him. With a 150-mile-per-hour prop wash, the force of the fan caused chunks of debris to hit the back of his neck.

"Ach!" Drake swiped the blood trickling over his shoulder.

He'd helped work on the boats as one of his odd jobs to earn food and supplies, but he wasn't used to piloting them. With no breaks on an airboat, he did his best to slow down and aim for the small dock near his home. The old wood planks had seen better days, and a corner was submerged in water. The boat drifted onto the shore next to the dock.

It would be easier to carry the woman if he shifted form, but Drake didn't want to frighten her if she awoke while he took her inside his small cabin home.

He slowly turned her onto her back. The subtle color shift on her forehead predicted the forming of a bruise. He touched the wound lightly. Her skin was soft.

Tradition had it that when he saw his mate, he'd know. At least that is what the elders claimed. The humans appeared to be much more unsure of the process. Why else would they get their marriage choices wrong so often? Perhaps humans did not have the same mating gene as the Draig.

Drake hefted the woman into his arms and hopped off the end of the boat onto the shore. She moaned, a soft, female sound. He tried to step lightly as not to jostle her.

His cabin was small, simple, but it reminded him of home — not like the busy streets of New Orleans' French Quarter where he'd first been introduced to Earth culture. The Louisiana swamps were a lot like the marshes near where he'd grown up. Well, except his homeland had small poisonous *givre* and Louisiana had giant alligators…and beautiful, stranded women.

A widow let him stay in the cabin in return for help whenever she needed it. Usually, that meant Ursa wanted someone to eat with her and help mow her lawn. Before coming to Earth, Drake had never mowed a lawn. It was strangely rewarding — like a mini harvesting where he was the giant plowing down tiny fields.

He might be spending too much time alone these days.

He placed the woman on his bed and studied her for a moment. It appeared very intimate to have her here, especially since she was missing pants. A man's bed was for a wife. He lifted her back up and moved her to the couch. Studying her again, he frowned. There wasn't as much space for her on the couch, and it felt wrong to give a woman an inadequate bed. Finally, he picked her up yet again and placed her back on his bed.

For a long moment, he stared at her. Now that he had her safe, he wondered what he should do with her. With her father now dead, she was clearly his responsibility. He'd need to do things for her. Provide. Feed her. Clothe her. Find her a suitable mate. Kill the unsuitable ones if they dared too much. It was a lot of responsibility. He'd never been a guardian before.

Kneeling beside the bed, he found himself enamored with her face. Perhaps he should kill any man who dared to come too close to her. The strong sense of protection he felt took him by surprise, but the gods had put her in his path for a reason. Hesitantly, he moved to caress her cheek. That's when he realized his shirtsleeve was soaked with blood, and he was a little lightheaded from the swamp battle.

Maybe resting for the moment would be his best course of action. Drake backed away from her, slumped against the bedroom wall and then slid down to the floor. He needed to watch over her anyway. Here would be as good of a place as any.

CHAPTER THREE

Lori didn't open her eyes as she pushed out of bed. More on autopilot than aware, she moved until her feet hit the floor. Morning was not her time to shine, but photoshoots often demanded she function before dawn. A slight headache settled around the back of her right eye, but she didn't think it was anything a vat of coffee wouldn't cure.

She rubbed her temple and reached forward to where her light switch should be as she finally peeked to see where she was going. The shock of unfamiliar wall hit her about the same time her foot accidently kicked an animal on the floor. She jumped back with a loud gasp. It took several moments for her to process that she stood in a strange bedroom in some kind of log cabin. The bed was covered with a large blue blanket embroidered with a silver dragon. It wasn't exactly what she'd expect to see in a cabin. Blinking hard, she tried to process her surroundings. She looked to the floor. It wasn't a dog, but a man slouched uncomfortably against the wall. His chest rose and fell in shallow breaths.

Lori kneeled beside him. She lifted his jaw and brushed a shock of dark hair off his face. Handsome features were made rugged by a scar along his temple and the slight stubble of his beard. His skin was hot to the touch.

"Mister?" She cradled his head and gave him a little shake. "Mister, can you wake up?" She frowned. What did the Cajuns who'd rented her the airboat call a man? "Um, *monsieur*? Mister? Dude? Guy bleeding on the floor wake your ass up?"

No answer, just the even rise and fall of his chest as he breathed. She glanced over his body, finding his arm covered in dried blood. When she tried to pull at his sleeve, it stuck to his skin. She remembered hallucinating what looked like a lizard man fighting an alligator. This, of course, was nothing as ridiculous as a lizard man, but the wound on his arm did make her think he was the man who'd rescued her in the swamps.

"Hello?" she yelled. "Is anyone here? We need a doctor. Hello?"

Lori's call went unanswered.

"Ok, then, mister. Let's get you on the bed and figure out what's wrong with you." Having a plan was much easier than implementing it. She braced her legs and slipped her arms around his torso, but no amount of willpower was going to help her muscles lift the over six foot tall, broad frame. "Shit." She rested him against the wall. "Don't worry, mister. I'll figure out something. You saved me from the swamp. I'm not going to let anything happen to you on my watch."

Lori went to the bed and pulled off the bedding and pillows. She laid them on the floor and then maneuvered the man onto the makeshift bed. It wasn't perfect, but at least he would be more comfortable. After she had finished, she studied her work. He lay on his back. His arms were at his sides. His legs were pulled straight.

Lori went in search of a first aid kit and telephone. The cabin home was sparse — a few pieces of sturdy furniture, a refrigerator and stove, a bathroom neatly supplied with masculine toiletries.

"Oh, great, I keep getting stranded with Cajuns in the middle of nowhere, and this one is trying to die on me, too. All I need is one stupid phone." She opened drawers and cabinets, frantically searching for anything that would help. "Come on, who doesn't have a phone in this century?"

Lori found washcloths, soap and hard liquor, but no medicines of any kind. As for a phone, she found an old house jack but nothing to plug into it. If this trip wasn't a warning against leaving her cell phone behind and going low tech, she wasn't sure what was.

Outside the airboat with Big Daddy's body had been pushed next to a broken dock, but there were no signs of vehicles of any kind. She wouldn't be driving him to a hospital.

"I really am stranded out here," she said, the fear building inside of her.

She returned to the bedroom and set to work cleaning the man's arm. Several punctures surrounded a long gash. Angry red skin lined the deep wound.

"This is for your own good," she said as she poured liquor over his arm to sanitize it before gently laying a washcloth over the gash. He didn't react. Lori searched his dresser and ended up tying the washcloth in place with a pair of his socks.

As soon as she finished tying the sock, he lifted his arm. Lori gasped and fell back. He studied the bandage and arched a brow. "Are you done burning me?"

"Burning…?" Lori glanced to the liquor bottle. "You were awake for that?"

"I've been awake since you stroked my legs." His voice was deep and sent a chill down her spine. She didn't recognize his accent, but it vaguely reminded her of a Scandinavian actor she'd seen on television once.

"Stroked...?" She looked at his leg. Had she touched him inappropriately when she'd moved him onto his back? "No, I wasn't..."

The man smiled.

"Why didn't you say something if you were awake?" she demanded.

His smile widened.

"I thought you were dying." She gestured to his arm.

He dropped his bandaged arm to his stomach. "I wanted to see what you were trying to do to me."

Lori looked down the man's body. She wasn't sure if he meant for his words to sound so sexual and inviting, but they were. She thought how easy it would be to climb over him and...

Think of a new topic, she ordered herself.

"You don't sound Cajun," she observed. "You don't even sound like you're from the South. What are you doing out here in the swamps?"

Ok, stupid topic, but better than salivating over him.

"I am," he answered. "I live here. This is the South. I am Cajun."

"No, I would say Scandinavian. Swedish? Norwegian?"

"Ursa said if anyone asked I am to say I am Cajun." He looked very sincere.

28

Lori felt a small tickle of apprehension. Logically, if someone was to say to her that they were trapped in a cabin in the middle of a nowhere swamp with a man claiming to be something he was not, with no technical conveniences, she'd tell them they had better run from a serial killer…or a really awful horror movie plot.

"Ursa?"

"She did a ceremony to make it official," he continued.

"A ceremony? To make you Cajun?"

"Yes."

"What kind of ceremony?"

"We had to drink a bottle of her moonshine and then I swam naked in the swamp while she watched from the shore."

"Oh, um, ok. My mistake. You're clearly Cajun." Lori waved her hand in dismissal, not wanting to delve into the craziness of that conversation. "We should get you to a hospital."

"I should provide you with something more appropriate to wear," he answered, as if to dismiss her suggestion that he should seek medical help.

Lori glanced down, seeing she wore a not-so-charming combination of mud and panties. "It covers as much as my swimsuit," she said, "but, yes, perhaps I should change."

"Yes. You wash. I will tend to your father."

"My father?"

"I heard you call that man your daddy. I am sorry you lost him in such a way." He pushed up to sit on the floor.

"Big Daddy is not my father. He was my swamp guide." Lori found herself staring at his facial scar, wondering how he'd received it.

"Then I should get Big Daddy to his people," the man said. "They will wish to honor his remains."

"Big Daddy can't be helped. You need a doctor to look at that arm and to keep it from getting infected. There could be nerve damage." She used the dresser to pull herself to her feet. He gestured to a drawer. Lori found a pair of athletic shorts inside. He watched as she pulled them over her legs.

"I should not have left him on the boat." The man stood.

"Whoa, easy, let the authorities take care of it. They might not like it if you move his body." Lori walked after him as he left the room.

"You have a strange way of showing respect to your dead," he stated.

"And you seem unable to admit you're sick and need to see a doctor," she answered. "That arm needs to be looked at."

He lifted it and studied the wound for a brief moment, a superficial gesture. "It is healing."

Lori again noted his old scar. "Is there a reason why you aren't one for medical care?"

"I do not need doctors," he stated matter-of-factly.

"Did something happen to make you not trust doctors? I'm not sure by your accent where you were before coming to America, but our health care system is very dependable and safe."

The man touched his cheek. "You keep eyeing my scar. This is not from last night. It does not need care."

"Oh, I didn't mean to stare." Lori forced her eyes away. "It seemed as if there might be a story there."

"On my home world, there was a disagreement with neighboring Var marsh farmers who wanted to steal part of my family's growing territory. When we refused and fought back, the Myrddin clan sent cat guards to intimidate us. They jumped out of the brush to attack us like cowards and this scar is the result of one of those raids."

"What happened?" Lori didn't remember hearing about the events he was talking about. "Did your family keep your land?"

"We petitioned the Draig royals to help us stop the attacks to our borders. The Myrddin clan denied it and, being as they are one of the oldest noble families on the planet, they were not questioned. Our royals brokered a deal with the Var royals, and we lost some of our family's property to the Var because they claimed to have found old territorial documents that proved it was their land, and we were trespassing. Never mind that my family had been growing on it since anyone could remember, and the validity of the documents could not be proven." The man sighed. "It is one of the reasons I left Qurilixen and came here."

Draig? Var? Qurilixen? These weren't people and places she recognized.

There was a sadness in him when he talked about it, but also a detachment as if he'd come to terms with whatever the past had given him. When he once more moved toward the airboat near a half-sunken dock, she grabbed his uninjured arm to stop him. "Just stop for a second."

He looked down at her hand. As much as she tried to ignore it, she felt attraction bubbling inside her. He narrowed his eyes and leaned closer. "You are not frightened by me?"

Lori shook her head in denial. "No. Why would I be? You saved me. I'm very grateful to you. I don't know why you were out on the swamps last night, but thank you for being there."

"I was tracking hunters. They've been causing trouble in the shadowed marshes. Forgive me, you call them swamps. I am told the hunters are probably drunkards acting without thought of their actions. They sit on their boat at night and shoot toward the shore. They almost shot me more than once, and I worry they will injure the next person. I thought your boat might be theirs." As if skeptical, he studied her carefully and questioned, "You feel it as well?"

Lori swallowed nervously at the abrupt change in conversation. She wanted to pretend she didn't know what he was talking about but couldn't bring herself to play coy. There was something between them, a very real connection that snapped through her fingers each time they touched. She gave a very weak, single nod. "You haven't told me your name."

"Here I am called Drake," he stated. "Ursa found me in the swamps and thought it a fitting name. She said if I was to be Cajun I needed a new name that people could pronounce."

"Ursa?" Lori wondered who this woman was to Drake. He had already mentioned her several times. It seemed strange that she would be jealous over someone she'd just met, but the feeling was there.

"She owns this property."

"And elsewhere you are called?" She gave him a small smile.

"Dimosthenis," he said, his accent thickening to make the word nearly impossible to attempt repeating. "But I am not to go by that anymore. I am Cajun now. That was my old life, and I left it behind."

"Nice to meet you, Drake. I'm Lori Johnston."

"We met last night and, it was not so nice," he stated.

Lori made a weak noise, unable to fault the literal translation of his logic. "So do you live here with family?"

A wife maybe? The last thing she wanted was to be attracted to a taken man.

"I have no family. I am the last of my bloodline."

"I'm sorry to hear that," she said, again sensing the loneliness in his statement.

"Then I will not tell you more. I have no wish to say things that displease you."

"No, I meant I'm sorry for your loss. It sounds by the tone of your voice that maybe you lost your family. You may tell me whatever you wish. I won't tell you not to speak." Lori started to reach for him but then pulled back.

"My family is dead. They did not make the journey to Louisiana with me. I left soon after my brother's death. He was killed by a cat."

"I'm sorry. It can't be easy to lose someone without warning, like to an animal attack."

"Why do you keep apologizing? None of these events was of your doing." Drake eyed her. "Unless you believe you are a god?"

"Nope. Not a god." Lori didn't bother to further that course of the conversation. Instead, she gestured to his bandaged arm. The sock wraps had loosened. "Please, let me take you to a doctor to have your arm looked at. You saved my life last night. The least you can do is let me save yours today."

He arched a brow.

"Infections can kill," Lori explained. "It might not be as terrifying a foe as an alligator, but I'm not going back in that swamp anytime soon if you decide to go swimming."

"It will be fine," he stated. "You may save my life another time if you so wish. But I agree you should not go into the swamps. Flailing in mud is not an acceptable form of combat."

Lori started to laugh, but Drake looked very earnest. "I'll try my best to remember that," she said.

"You were not trained very well. If you like, I will show you proper survival skills in case you are trapped again on an airboat in the swamps."

"Thank you for the offer, but I'm pretty sure that won't be happening again." She wasn't sure what the fates had in mind by bringing her to his doorstep, but she was very curious to see where their budding friendship might go. Even though he spoke in clipped words and had very solemn expressions, she felt as if she understood him on a natural, unspoken level.

Chapter Four

Finally. The gods had blessed him. Drake had found his mate. His one true wife.

They were meant to be together. Lori knew it as well. She'd said as much. She felt their connection.

Drake wanted to smile and shout to the cypress trees how happy he was to have finally found the woman destined to be his. It was just as the Draig elders had said it would be. When he'd opened his eyes that morning to find her tending him, he'd known. Something inside him had burst forth. However, with his somber responsibility to deliver the dead man to his family, Drake had to try very hard to remain calm.

There was not much he could do to prepare Big Daddy beyond wrapping him in a shroud. When he finished, he found Lori waiting for him near the house. She had just showered, and the mud was off her body. As she'd bathed, he had stripped off everything except for the arm bandage she'd made for him and rinsed off with a hose so he wouldn't smell like the swamps. He slid on a pair of stiff jeans that had dried on the clothes line.

"Ursa will have a way to contact the authorities to bring the man home," he said. "I radioed her to send help. Now we wait."

"Why don't you radio authorities yourself?" she asked. Her eyes were on his naked chest, and he glanced down wondering why she stared at him with such a strange expression.

"My radio only goes to Ursa," he stated.

"This Ursa really keeps you under her thumb, doesn't she?" Lori muttered.

"I do not—" He started to ask her to explain the comment, but she cut him off.

"I don't see a vehicle. Do you have a way to drive out of here?" Her eyes finally lifted to meet his.

"No need. I swim or run when I need to go somewhere."

"What about a phone?"

"No need. I have a radio."

"That only goes to Ursa," she clarified. "You are living off the grid, aren't you?"

"Unfortunately, though this grid looks similar to home, I cannot survive solely off the land here." He lifted the black device he'd found in the boat. "Does this flashing weapon belong to you?"

Lori chuckled and reached to take it. "I have never heard my camera referred to as a weapon before, but I suppose there is power in images."

He enjoyed her smile. Their fingers touched, and he found himself unable to let go of the device. Instead, he used her hold on it to pull her closer. The magnetism of her body was unlike anything he'd experienced. His heart quickened like when on a hunt. His stomach tightened like in the lonely hours of the night. His mouth tingled for contact.

Drake had seen mating couples, knew what was to happen, but he'd never had the opportunity or inclination to touch a woman. Now the emotion was like a force of nature. He couldn't help himself. Instinct took over, and he leaned his mouth to hers.

Heat infused him at the intimate contact, warming the full length of his body in a way the hot Louisiana sun could not. She made a soft sound. He broke the kiss to study her face.

Lori breathed heavily. Her eyes were closed, and she took several breaths before she opened them to look at him. "Why did you stop?"

"You protested," he answered. "Honor dictates that I do not overstep. There are rules. No matter how badly I want to kiss you, if you protest, I—"

"That wasn't a protest, Drake." She wrapped her arms around his neck. "Not even close."

CHAPTER FIVE

Lori wasn't sure what made her drop all inhibitions. She wasn't foolish. Logically, she knew what she felt might be gratitude to her rescuer. Drake had saved her from the swamp.

But so what if she was grateful? He was also a handsome man who had enough kindness to help a stranger.

Plus, he had really strong lips.

Firm, strong lips.

Firm, strong, sexy lips.

What could one kiss hurt?

She pulled his mouth to hers, bringing him back into the kiss. He hesitated before touching her hips to draw her closer. The firm muscles of his body crashed into hers in full reality. The shock of complete contact made her forget everything but that moment. He slid his tongue across her lips, not dipping forward, but testing to see if she would resist.

Lori mimicked his movement before deepening the kiss. Every nerve sparked to awareness. One kiss turned into one touch, which turned into one grasp, one caress, and then another, and another…another.

Mindlessly, she continued kissing him. Her hands delved into his hair. She felt her body being lifted from the ground, but reason did not register.

Drake carried her inside the cabin. The window air-conditioning unit had dropped the temperature several degrees, but the heat from his body kept her warm. When her feet again touched the floor, she thought about pulling away, of doing the sensible thing. She knew she should stop what was happening.

Logic couldn't override her need to be next to him. It was a primal emotion, an invisible pull that brought her gaze to his, her lips to his, her body to his. The light danced strangely in his eyes with an inner glow that entranced even as it fascinated.

"This doesn't make sense," she whispered.

"The will of the gods doesn't have to."

It was either the strangest or the sweetest thing a man had ever said to her.

Drake kissed her, cutting off any weak protest she might have tried to lay voice to. He walked her to the side of the bed. The mattress hit the back of her legs as he pressed her against it. His hands roamed over her sides and hips before cupping her ass.

"Condom?" Lori whispered as he lifted her onto the mattress.

"You are very beautiful." Drake tugged at her clothing, easily pulling the athletic shorts off her hips. The shirt was soon to follow. His eyes pierced into hers, so intense she had to glance away. Heat radiated off him. His breathing deepened. The hypnotic pull of his naked chest drew her like nothing she'd ever experienced. With each touch, she fell deeper under his spell.

Lori didn't believe in mindless desire or irrational decisions made in the heat of passion, but here she was stripping pants off a man she'd just met. She was careful not dislodge the bandage she'd made on his arm. Her hands trembled as she touched his hips. The tip of his naked arousal brushed against her.

"Condom?" she asked again. She was on birth control for pregnancy but prided herself on making good choices when it came to sex.

"You are very beautiful," he answered hoarsely.

His kisses became aggressive as he pushed her back on the bed. The feel of his body over hers made it nearly impossible to concentrate. He touched everywhere he could reach, following his hands with an eager mouth as if he couldn't explore her body fast enough, as if there were so many things to discover. She wanted him to slow, and yet there was something endearing in the enthusiasm he displayed.

"It's not a race," Lori said, chuckling as she tried to pull his mouth from her breast.

Drake lifted his head to look at her. "We will have festivities to celebrate our joining later. We may host a race if you wish. I will comply with all of your people's customs. I know there must be flowers and cake."

"You mean a date?" Lori couldn't help laughing. Festivities?

"If you wish it to be formal we will set a date for the festivities. Whatever you desire, love, I will make happen."

Love? She began to laugh again only stopped when she saw his serious expression. He looked as if he desperately wanted to start kissing her again but was waiting for permission to continue.

Trying not to sound critical, she probed, "How long have you been in this country? You speak English very well."

"I came through the portal a few years ago. The gods sent me to New Orleans." He gave a distasteful grimace. "I thought at first I was being punished for leaving home and had landed here to serve the penance of afterlife. The air smelled of human waste, and several of the people were diseased. The first night of my arrival, one woman warned of the LaLaurie spirits trapped in a large temple. They should leave the angry spirits offerings. Perhaps then the city would not be so cursed."

"Diseased?" Lori took a deep breath. This was an odd conversation, to be sure, and definitely not the most romantic. She couldn't help moving her legs restlessly against his thighs. He held himself very rigid.

"Yes, they were losing their meals in the cracked streets and dancing erratically. I do not know if the unbalance was a plague or the spell of the pipers as they played. Either way, I have never imaged diseased people to be so happy. Perhaps the musician doctors were doing what they could for them. The music medicine was strange to me, but the players were very talented. It was one thing I enjoyed of the city. The food smelled delightful, but I did not eat for I did not wish to join the locals in their torture."

It took Lori a moment to process, especially since he was naked on top of her having this weird conversation. She breathed heavily, trying very hard to concentrate on his words. It was a little hard to follow his command of the English language. The ache inside her body intensified as he settled against her. "Oh, you mean you were in the French Quarter during the party hours."

"Yes, I believe Ursa also said the people had the plague of the French Quarters. Apparently, people from your home world pilgrimage there to suffer. It makes no sense to me, but I cannot judge the humans' rite of passage. My home world was cursed in its own way, but not to the depths of the French Quarters. For reasons unknown to my people—at least the common people, since the royals were never forthcoming about the problem—female children aren't being conceived, and my generation has very little to choose from when it comes to finding a wife. It was one of the reasons I left. There was no future for me there."

Lori was caught somewhere between laughter and confusion. Not that what he said was funny, so much as how he said it and his timing for the conversation. Musician doctors? Home world? She knew she should say something, but for the life of her all she wanted to do was kiss the crazy man and make him finish what they'd started.

He took a deep, unsteady breath. "Have you any other questions for me? I will answer them all dutifully, but I would very much like to continue what we were doing."

"Oh," Lori glanced down between their bodies. The ripple of his muscles hovered close to her stomach.

Desire churned between them, and she couldn't help lifting her hips. "I didn't mean for you to stop and —"

"Then you are sure you want this?" he clarified.

Lori reached for his chest and rubbed her palms over his tight flesh. "I am here willingly, and thank you for being respectful enough to ask."

A dam inside him appeared to break open, flooding out in a torrent of emotions. He kissed her passionately as if his very life depended on breathing her in. He stroked the curve of her hip and thigh, urging her legs to part for him. That first brush of intimate contact caused her to stiffen in anticipation.

This was really happening.

All thoughts escaped but the primitive drive of her body. Without realizing it, she had been starving her primal needs, and now they took over, bursting forth and demanding to be satiated. Ironically, she had told him to slow down. Now he did not go fast enough. She needed to feel more, needed him inside her.

Lori pushed Drake onto his back and straddled his waist. Grabbing his face, she kissed him, rubbing her tongue against his. Her hips worked over his, angling into the perfect position until she finally slid down on top of him. The fullness caused an involuntary jerk, and she gasped. Drake held her waist, keeping her body from retreating. He held her tightly to him, rocking deep. She gazed down at his passion-laden eyes.

Oh, fuck. This is really happening.

Nothing could have stopped her from moving on top of him. The need became desperate, demanding. She needed to feel him, needed to find that perfect moment of release.

Oh, fuck. Oh, fuck.

Lori met a hard climax and couldn't move. For a second, tension seized hold only to roll away in glorious waves of pleasure. Drake cried out and gripped her tightly.

As the tremors lessened, reason flooded back. She looked down to their joined bodies. Lori pushed up, the logical fighting to take over the primal now that she'd found release. "Oh, no."

His expression changed from one of pleasure to concern.

"We forgot protection. We shouldn't have done that." She stood and gave him a wary look.

"I don't understand. Why would you need protection? Is someone out to harm you? The hunters…?"

"What?" She shook her head. "No, protection against STDs."

He arched a brow, clearly still not understanding.

"Sexually transmitted diseases," she clarified. "For what it's worth, I shouldn't get pregnant, and all my blood tests have come back fine." She gave him an expectant look.

"You believe because I was in New Orleans I will disease you?" Drake slowly sat on the bed. "I assure you, I am honorable."

"It's nothing personal. You know how it is these days. The free-love movement is over. Now you have to—"

"You wish for me to secure a bride price for you?"

Lori laughed. How could she not? "Marriage? Oh God, no. I think what I'm saying is lost in translation. No, I'm not asking you to marry me. That would be ridiculous. I meant we shouldn't have had sex without a condom."

"I told you, you are very beautiful," he stated. "Why do you keep asking for me to repeat this? Do you think my word will change?"

"I, um…what?"

"You keep ordering me to compliment you."

"Condom?"

"Yes, you are beautiful. You smell nice. I like your skin. What is this ultimate compliment that you seek?"

"Condoms are what you wrap around your penis to prevent disease transmission and pregnancy."

"I think you are mistaken. The sign with the smiling woman says, *Condoms: Pay her the Ultimate Compliment.*"

"That's an advertisement," Lori said. "It means wear a condom."

Drake suddenly stood. He appeared angry. "You keep saying I'm diseased, and you do not wish to carry my son."

"I am so confused right now." Lori felt vulnerable standing naked before him. She reached for her borrowed shirt and shorts.

"What's done is done, you cannot change it." He apparently had no problem standing in nothing but an arm bandage.

Seeing his naked form made it hard to look directly at him. She wanted to forget this conversation, crawl back into his bed and start over. "I'm not saying I regret sleeping with you. I'm just saying that we should have thought about—"

"Are you, or are you not, my bride?"

That was the second time he'd mentioned marriage.

"We have fulfilled my people's customs. We have stated our intention to be together and have mated. I believe you require a ceremony of flowers and cake. I have seen Ursa's pictures."

Lori really wanted to meet this Ursa, who apparently liked filling Drake's head with half-explained nonsense.

"Oh, ah, we are not engaged to be married," she stated. That much needed to be clear. Would she consider dating him? Yes. Would she consider sleeping with him again? Yes, as long as they got past this little bout of crazy. Would she agree to get pregnant with his love child without a serious commitment and careful planning? No. The logistics of a potential relationship were confusing—he didn't have a phone or internet, and she didn't live in the area.

"I see." Drake grabbed a pair of jeans from a drawer and strode from the room. She watched his naked ass as he passed through the door. "I hear the sheriff's car."

Lori followed him but didn't hear anything.

***

Drake didn't understand what had happened. They were mated, weren't they? At least according to his people's custom. They'd both agreed and then shared a bed. That meant something. All right, so his cabin was no Draig marriage tent, and he hadn't presented her to the dragon king and queen, but surely allowances could be made being as he was on an entirely new planet.

This was a test. It had to be a test.

But why? The facts were simple and unmistakable. Drake had found her. She'd agreed. They'd mated. The end. They were married according to the most fundamental of Draig traditions. Already he felt his body completely focused on her, each nerve reaching to join hers. Each thought ached to reach into her mind and communicate.

He'd seen her that first night on the boat, felt her familiarity even though he didn't know why at the time, and he'd innately known. That was how it worked. One second was all he'd needed to feel their bond, and he had given her hours to decide—plenty of time. So then why was she acting like they were nothing?

Drake walked out onto his lawn. His shifter hearing had picked up the sheriff's car about five miles down the road. As much as he wanted to present his mate to witnesses, a somewhat traditional gesture to finalize marriages, he maintained his distance. If she didn't want to be with him, maybe he could undo the mating process. If he didn't tell a witness that he'd slept with her…

Seeing her on his porch staring at him, he knew it was too late. He had found his woman, and she no longer wanted him. The warrior in him wanted to fight for her, to demand she love him, stay with him, mate with him. The dragon in him wanted to snatch her and hide her away until she realized what he already did. The man in him knew he was honor bound to respect her word and not force himself on her if she no longer wanted him.

The gods had been exact and cruel in his punishment. He had left home, defied the royals' plan, and now he was paying the ultimate price — never to be fully mated and banished forever from his childhood home world.

CHAPTER SIX

Lori was torn between her photo-journalistic instincts to lift her camera and take pictures of the police and emergency workers as they took possession of Big Daddy's remains, and her need to respect the privacy of the man who'd lost his life while taking her around the swamps. In the end, she only took a few tasteful shots of the event. The idea to write a human-interest piece paying homage to Big Daddy's life on the swamp was already swirling in her head. It was the least she could do, given the circumstances.

Drake did not speak to her, but she did catch him watching her intently. Sheriff Jackson had arrived alone in his older sedan model police car. He took a few pictures on his cell phone, called someone and then ordered the paramedics—Chester and Jim—to take the body away.

"Don't you need a medical examiner out here to...?" Lori's words trailed off as the sheriff gave her a you're-not-from-these-parts-are-you? look. The man spoke in low tones to Drake, gestured to the swamp a few times, gestured toward her a few times, wrote a few things down and then closed his notebook. Case closed, apparently.

"Excuse me," Lori called, running after one of the paramedics. Chester, the younger paramedic, looked new to the field, but he and his partner had appeared competent in what they were doing… Well, as far as could be observed when the patient they were attending to had already passed away. She touched his arm and gently led him to where Drake stood by the sheriff. "Like I mentioned when you arrived, I need you look at Drake's arm. He was bitten by an alligator trying to save me."

"He said it's fine," Chester stated. "I can't—"

"Listen, ah—" Lori paused and glanced around at the men who now all focused their attention on her, " — Chester, you can either look at it and make me happy, or I can follow you around nagging until you give in."

"I…" Chester looked at Drake. "Please show me your arm."

The sheriff chuckled. He was a salt-'n-pepper type with the kind of weathered face seen in cowboy movies. His gravelly voice and thick almost hard-to-understand Southern accent would have been intimidating if not for his easy smile. "Go on, Drake. You better do what she says. I have what I need from you."

Drake nodded once. Without speaking, he lifted his arm to the paramedic and met Lori's gaze.

Chester arched a brow as he untied the socks of her makeshift bandage.

"I wrapped it," she said, "but I'm worried about an infection. He won't go to a doctor. Maybe if you tell him, he'll listen."

Drake's eyes stayed focused on her. There was a possessiveness in them that caused a small shiver to wash over her. She hadn't liked where they'd left their conversation, but she wasn't sure what else she could say. He apparently wanted the ultimate commitment. She wasn't going to marry him and have a baby after one night. To even consider it would be insane.

Still, she couldn't explain the ache inside her when she thought of leaving his home and never seeing him again. There was something between them, potent and real. Just looking at him made her heart beat faster. She wanted to touch him. She wanted to hear his strange stories about landing in New Orleans and misunderstanding the French Quarter, stories of what he called his home world, where there were royals and man-eating cats and a low female population.

The paramedic dropped the bandage on the ground and examined the wounded arm. It doesn't look that bad to me." He moved the wrist and elbow. "Any tenderness?"

Drake shook his head in denial.

"Follow up with the doctor if you want, but—" Chester began.

"Not bad?" Lori made a small sound of surprise. Was the man an idiot? She stepped closer to look for herself. "Are you looking at the right arm? The man clearly needs stitches and medical…" Her words trailed off as she looked at Drake's arm. The deep gashes had disappeared. "But, no, I saw…" She reached for his other arm and lifted it to check that they'd examined the right one. "But there was blood and…"

"Doesn't look like it broke the skin, but you can use antibiotic ointment on it if you want. I think you'll survive," Chester told Drake a little sarcastically before glancing at Lori. He looked as if he wished to say a great many things but held back.

"Drake, are you sure you don't need to go to the hospital?" the sheriff asked.

"No, I'm not injured," Drake stated.

Lori kept staring at Drake's arm, studying the pink scratches as if the gashes would somehow come back.

With a curt nod to the sheriff, Chester said, "Jackson," by way of a parting acknowledgment, and left.

"Drake, I saw your arm. There's blood on the towel. That came from —" Lori realized she still gripped Drake's arm, and she let him go. "I'm not crazy. You were hurt. I saw —."

"I understand you had a difficult night, Miss Johnston," Sheriff Jackson interrupted. "I'll give you a ride to the station. We'll take your statement there and then get you back to your hotel just as quickly as possible. I'm sure you'll want to put this entire experience behind you." He turned to Drake. "Can I trust you'll get the airboat back to where it needs to go? Big Daddy is a fixture several miles upstream at Gator Boat Rides. The Beauchamps are good people. If you bring it back, they'll give you a ride home. Or do you want me to have the owners send someone out?"

"I'll take care of it. They will have enough duties to attend to with the passing of their loved one," Drake said.

"Always liked that about you," the sheriff drawled. "Might not have been born in the swamp like the rest of us, but you understand the way things should be." Then, to Lori he said, "Come on, miss."

"Drake," Lori began, unsure what to say. She looked at his lips, wanting to rewind time to when they were alone in his room before she had a mini responsibility freak-out. But that was impossible. He was some good ole boy living in the swamp, who swam with alligators, and she was from civilization. As much as she wanted to wrap her arms around his neck and kiss him, she knew it was best she didn't linger. There was so much she wanted to say, but the sheriff was staring at her expectantly. Instead, she said, "Thank you for saving me. I can never repay you for that." She started to leave but then stopped. "I'm at the Plantation Inn for the next few days. If you come by, I'd like to buy you dinner—" she glanced at Sheriff Jackson, who continued to watch her intently, "—as a thank you. I know it's not much, but…"

Drake nodded. "If it is what the gods will, I will see you again."

Right. The gods. It wasn't exactly the enthusiastic answer she'd been hoping for.

Lori felt the sheriff leading her by the arm to his car. He opened the passenger-side door and let her sit in the front seat. She turned to stare at Drake out of the window. He didn't move, merely stood, watching her go.

"Don't be offended if he doesn't come to dinner, miss," the sheriff said as he started the engine. "These swamp boys tend to stick to their own."

The man didn't outright say she didn't fit in, but he didn't have to. She already knew. Any kind of relationship would be impossible. Drake didn't have a phone, so a long-distance relationship was out of the question, and she wasn't about to move into gator village. The best she could hope for was that his gods willed them to meet again in a different reality.

As the car moved through the thick trees, Drake's cabin was instantly hidden. The roads twisted and turned until she was sure she'd never be able to find it again. Lori turned her attention to the camera in her lap. The battery was nearly dead, so she slowly placed it in her bag.

Considering where she'd been last night, she should be happy to be on her way back to civilization. Yet, as the car put miles between herself and Drake, she couldn't help feeling an immense loss. It knotted her stomach and caused an actual pain to linger in her chest near her heart. There had been something between them, an undeniable connection, and their brief moment together had been cut too short.

CHAPTER SEVEN

The police station secretary typed with two fingers—two very slow henpecking fingers. The sheriff hadn't lied when he'd said taking Lori's statement would be quick and painless. What he'd failed to point out was Darla was very fond of her manicure, and Lori couldn't leave until she'd signed the finished document.

"Unlike the stuff in most stations, our coffee's not bad," Sheriff Jackson said, handing her a disposable coffee cup and a donut on a napkin. He'd let her wait in his office on a brown leather couch. "And no cop-donut jokes. My brother owns a bakery."

"Thank you," Lori answered, grateful. She gave him a small smile. "And I don't joke about a good donut."

The sheriff glanced to where her camera battery was charging in the plugin. He took a small sip of his own coffee before setting it on his desk. "Photographer, eh?"

He knew as much. She'd said so in her statement. But Lori appreciated his efforts at small talk and nodded. "Yes." She went to retrieve her battery and began setting up her camera to look at the photos. "Originally, I came to write a travel piece on Plantation Inn. I wanted to get a few shots of the swamps in the evening light. I still owe that review to my editor, but after everything that has happened, I feel I need to do something for Big Daddy…and for Drake."

"Drake?" The sheriff arched a brow and moved to shut his office door. It was a strange gesture considering the officers outside were not being loud.

"He saved me." Lori turned on the camera and began flipping through her shots. There were several of the inn and the owners.

"But why would you want to do a story on him?"

"Because he saved me," Lori repeated, looking up from the digital display of a breakfast buffet. "And he's a rather unique character. I think people will be interested in his story."

"Did you discuss this idea with him?"

Lori shook her head. "No, but I think good deeds deserve some kind of recognition, don't you? And it's a great story — the writer's personal experience, the fear of the swamps at night, the joy Big Daddy had in life right up until the end, hungry alligators and then the lizard man."

"Lizard man?" Sheriff Jackson crossed his arms and sat on his desk. He glanced out the office window to where three officers leaned over a file before turning back to study her.

"That's what I'll call it, 'Lizard Man of the Bayou'," Lori said. Next, she could write the story of how Drake had come to be in America. She'd first have to figure out where Qurilixen was, and who the Var and Draig were. They were probably a foreign language pronunciation for some Scandinavian village. When people heard royal families were taking away commoner land like it was still the medieval period, they'd be angry. Lori would bring notice to the cause.

She flipped faster through her pictures. There were several of Big Daddy and the swamps. A photographer teacher had once told her to shoot everything and plenty of it because film is cheap compared to a lost moment, and that's what Lori did.

"I'm not sure a story is a very good idea."

"Does the title need something more? Maybe I'll call it, 'Lizard Man of the Bayou: Stranded with a Cajun'," Lori mused.

"You were there one night. That's hardly stranded," the sheriff said.

"It sounds more dramatic that way," Lori answered. "And I was stranded in the swamps when he saved me."

"And Drake is not Cajun," the sheriff continued.

"He said he is," Lori defended. "Big Daddy was. Never mind. Simply, 'Lizard Man of the Bayou' it is."

"Listen, Drake is..." The sheriff paused as if measuring his words. "Well, he's a private person."

"I'm not going to print his home address," Lori said. She'd finally found a shot of alligator eyes lit up by her camera flash. The fear came over her once more, and also the immense relief that her trials in the swamp were over.

"We don't need people roaming the swamps looking for –"

"Lizard man," Lori whispered.

"Exactly," the sheriff agreed.

She blinked hard, staring at the camera. A lizard-like creature leaned over Big Daddy's dead body. Yellow reptilian eyes glared in annoyance as if her flash had interrupted him. His skin appeared to be armor plated like a dinosaur, with a line pushing up the center of his forehead to create a plate over his brow and nose. Talons replaced fingertips. She flipped the frame forward. He was still there. This time, she saw the glint of fanged teeth. She flipped again, and again the lizard man was there. The unmistakable line of a scar drew over his face, just like… "Drake."

"What?"

"Drake," she said, stunned. She blinked hard as if doing so would adjust her eyesight. He'd touched her. That mouth had kissed her. That body had been…inside her. "Drake is the lizard man."

"Let me see that," the sheriff said. The hard, authoritative tone made her stunned brain automatically obey. As he looked at her camera, he cursed lightly under his breath.

"He's…he's…" Lori stood and moved to look over the sheriff's shoulder.

Sheriff Jackson stepped away from her as he looked at her pictures. She tried to move behind him once more, and he again shifted positions. After a long moment, he handed the camera back. "You must be tired. I don't see anything."

"What…wait," Lori flipped through her pictures. The ones of Drake leaning over Big Daddy were gone. "No, I saw them. They were here. They were…" Her words trailed off as realization dawned. "You erased them. Why?"

"I don't know what you're talking about," Sheriff Jackson stated. "You must be tired from your ordeal.

City girl like you in the swamps at night. It's understandable."

But that was a lie. She saw it in his expression. Lori knew what she'd seen on her camera. "Why would you do that? There was proof of — "

"All I saw was proof of a woman stranded and scared in a place she doesn't belong," the sheriff interrupted. Gone was his friendly smile.

"What is this? Is this some kind of lizard town? Are you...?" She eyed the man, trying to see if his face would change, or his eyes would glow. She'd seen Drake's eyes glow. She'd thought it was a trick of the light, but until a minute ago, she hadn't had any proof he wasn't human. He was a lizard shape-shifter. That meant...shape-shifters existed. Supernaturals existed. And she was the first person to photograph one.

The sheriff smiled tightly as if putting on a show for anyone who'd glance into his office. He took her by the arm and squeezed in warning. "Listen very carefully. Drake is a good man. He saved your life. He's saved a lot of lives around here. You said thank you to him for his help, and that's the end of it. You're going to go home, write your travel article about the inn, and Drake won't so much as get a mention."

"You can't do this. You can't tell me what to write. This isn't Nazi Germany." She lifted her chin, hoping she sounded brave. "I have freedom of the press."

"And I have a badge." He tightened his grip. "I also have the number of the local mental health director at the hospital. If you keep talking about this, I'll have you locked up for observation due to exposure to the elements and psychological distress. I'll make a notation of it in my official report. So if you get any ideas, I'll say you're crazy, and we feared a mental breakdown, but that I let you go because you promised to seek medical help from your doctor when you returned home. Who do you think the public will believe? A travel reporter ranting about lizard men or a decorated man of the law? And if you think I'm bad, you should see the other folk Drake has helped. People here know the price of a life debt, and they're willing to pay it."

"But—"

"There is no such thing as a lizard man," the sheriff stated.

"But—"

"Say it. There is no such thing as a lizard man."

"There is no such thing as a lizard man," Lori whispered, shaking with fear.

"Good girl." He let her go. "Now sign your statement, and I'll have one of my officers bring you back to the inn. Your car is being picked up from the airboat rental parking lot and will be waiting for you when you get there."

Lori rubbed her arm and backed out of the man's way. She didn't appreciate being bullied. This might be the swamp, and they might have their weird swamp-people culture here, but she was a journalist. Sure, she was a travel journalist, but still, she had the right to publish what truths she wanted. Plus, she had one thing these backwater people clearly hadn't heard of—GPS metadata and automatic cloud backup for her photos.

CHAPTER EIGHT

"No. I cannot give you a ride to Plantation Inn. You need to stay away from her, Drake," the sheriff stated firmly. "She knows your secret, and she wants to expose you. Don't give her more ammunition to do so."

Drake stood, arms crossed, as he stared at the man. He did not believe Lori would try to harm him. Even now, he felt as if she was a part of him. The touch of her skin was imprinted on his body. The smell of her stayed in his nose. The sound of her echoed in his head. Watching her drive away had been agony, and he wanted to get her back. "Others know and—"

"Drake, listen. She's not one of us. She's an outsider. I managed to delete the photos she took of you, but you have to be more careful. I told you about cameras and the internet. All it takes is one online rumor to go viral, and people from all over the world will be down here trying to find the lizard man. It will become a fuck fest of new-age paranormal investigating assholes."

"I don't know what that means." Drake trusted the sheriff. The man had never lied to him. There was much about Earth that Drake had yet to learn. Still, he couldn't see Lori causing him problems. She might not want to be his wife, but surely she wouldn't try to intentionally harm him.

"It means your quiet life here will be disrupted. It means we'll have hundreds of idiots out in the swamps trying to catch you. If you think drunk rednecks on the water popping off shots at the shoreline is bad, wait until they start hunting you for real." The man sighed heavily. "About six years back, some kid staged a photo of a ghost in an abandoned home over on Bebette Road, made up some legend of the Bebette monster with directions on how to find it. We still get trespassers out there. Last winter, a group broke in to the wrong home and was almost shot by the owners. Two winters ago, a couple idiots got lost in the forest, and we had to send out search parties. One stupid picture, and now I have a lifetime of headaches."

"And idiots on the swamp looking for me means more accidents," Drake concluded.

"Yes. If you think tourist season is bad, you haven't seen anything. These idiots will start fishing for gators, trying to find you in the water."

Drake frowned. "That's not good."

"No. Not good. Idiots will get themselves eaten, and suddenly outsiders will call for all alligators to be put down like it was the animal's fault. There are a lot of people who owe their livelihood to hunting the swamps. It's a delicate balance."

Drake frowned, understanding the implication of what the sheriff was trying to tell him. If he went to see Lori, it could be the end of everything he'd come to know on Earth. It seemed preposterous that love could be so damaging, but who was Drake to argue with a man who understood humans in a way Drake could not?

"Let me talk to her. I can explain this." Drake had given his relationship with her a lot of thought. She'd invited him to dinner, and he had every intention of showing up. Well, every intention until the sheriff had appeared.

"Drake, trust me when I say privacy is better than the kind of attention that woman can bring you. Don't give her anything else to write about." He lowered his voice. "Forget the paranormal crowd. What about the government? You know what they'll do to you if they discover an alien is living in the Louisiana swamps. I showed you those articles and videos. Do you remember?"

"Yes. Area 51. Roswell. I do not understand why the Reticulans were treated so poorly. They are great ambassadors of medicine. They have cured many planets. I thought Draig royals were misguided, but your government..." Drake shook his head in disapproval. "I have no wish to be probed."

"Then please listen when I tell you this is for the best." The man clasped Drake's arm. "I'm not married, and I don't have any kids. All I have is my brother's family. When you saved my grand-niece from drowning after she wandered off from her mama, I promised you I would do everything in my power to protect your secret. Please, let me keep my word. Stay away from that woman. I can manage a few tourists and the locals, but even I can't stop the US government."

"I wish to give her flowers and cake," Drake said. "I love her. Lori is my life mate. I have connected to her."

The sheriff sighed. "Oh, son, it's like I've told you. Earth isn't like your home world. Earth women are not like dragon women. Even without your secret, a woman like Lori Johnston would never go for a swamp boy like you. You found your place here with us. She comes from an entirely different world. What you need is a good bayou woman who isn't afraid of a couple gator

72

bites, if ya catch my meaning." The sheriff gave a small wink.

"I don't understand. You said humans have not figured out intergalactic travel. What planet is she from?"

"Planet Yankee." Sheriff Jackson laughed.

Drake furrowed his brow. "Ursa told me of Yankees. Is that humor?"

"You're not laughing, so apparently not very good humor." The sheriff let go of him. "You have the ideal situation here, Drake. No one bothers you. No one asks questions. You don't pay taxes because legally you don't exist. You're living the dream."

"But I love her," Drake said.

"No one I know ever died of a broken heart," the sheriff answered. "You're young. You'll find it again."

Drake arched a brow. He was well aware that he looked to be a human thirty when in reality he was a Draig sixty-one. "I'm older than you are."

"Only by a couple years," the sheriff said. His wrinkled face shifted into a smile. "Us young guys have plenty of time."

Chapter Nine

"Welcome back, Miss Lori. How'd ya like the bayou?" Apparently, no one had told Janice, the Plantation Inn proprietor, what had happened.

"My tour guide died, and I was rescued by the lizard man," Lori answered.

Janice erupted into a very girlish display of giggles. "Oh, you! You're such a riot."

"I do try to entertain," Lori drawled. It was best she leave before the poor woman got the blunt end of Lori's bad mood. "Excuse me."

"So you saw him?" A Southern gentleman interrupted. He sat a book down next to his chair and stood. The foyer was cozy, and double doors opened to screened porch. His polo shirt and khaki pants were a clean-cut contrast to Lori's borrowed T-shirt and athletic shorts. The last thing she wanted was to stop and have a conversation while dressed like she'd woken up naked in the middle of a frat house.

Lori glanced at Janice and then back to the man.

"Miss Lori, this is Mr. Howards. He's a world traveler just back from Africa. Isn't that exciting?" Janice introduced. "And this is Miss Lori. She's a photographer. She's writing a feature on my little piece of heaven."

"What were you doing in Africa?" Lori asked.

"Big game hunting.

Lori tried not to look disgusted. "Is that even still legal?"

The man laughed but didn't answer.

"So what brings you to Louisiana?" Lori tried to be polite but didn't really care about the answer.

"Business. Pleasure." He shrugged lightly.

"Well, it was nice to meet you," Lori turned to leave, but his words stopped her. Apparently, the awkward conversation wasn't over.

"You were on the bayou?" he asked.

"Yes."

"Whereabouts?"

"Gator Boat Rides, wasn't it?" Janice inserted, trying to stay a part of the conversation. "We have brochures if you're interested."

"Yes, thank you," Mr. Howards answered.

"Actually, I'm not sure they'll be open. My guide had a heart attack last night and, unfortunately, didn't make it. I'd be surprised if they open up for business today." Lori stepped away from them. "Please, excuse me. It's been a long night."

"You mentioned a lizard man?" Mr. Howards insisted. "Were you at the swamps taking pictures? I would love to see them."

"There is no such thing as a lizard man," Lori stated, a little too harshly.

"Of course," he conceded. "Have a pleasant day, Miss Lori."

Lori took her opportunity leave and quickly moved to the carpeted stairs to go to her room.

"Speaking of the lizard man," Janice said, following her to the second floor. "I was talking to an old woman I know who sells jams at the farmers' market. She knows all about the lizard man legends. If you like to speak to her, I can get you her information."

"Um, yeah, sure, thanks," Lori answered. She wasn't sure what she was going to do about Drake. He'd saved her life. And, as much as she resented being told what to do by a backwater sheriff, she didn't want to bring Drake harm. Exposing him might do just that. Journalistic tendencies came a far second to Drake's wellbeing.

"But you'll mention the lizard man?" Janice insisted.

"I'm not sure."

"Miss Lori, please." Janice's tone begged for attention.

Lori stopped in the hall outside her room and turned to the woman.

"A local legend would be great for businesses. You said you wanted local culture. I'm not asking you to make anything up or write anything you're not comfortable with. Just, if you could, please mention the possibility of the lizard man. It would be greatly appreciated. We're having lizard-man T-shirts made up, coffee mugs. My son is building a website."

A day ago, Lori would have said yes without issue. The inn was adequate as far as accommodations and the staff was very polite. Janice had the kind of bubbly personality needed to run a small inn. But now Lori knew the lizard man was real. Drake was real. "I'll have to pass it by my editor, but I promise to see what I can do."

"Thank you!" Janice gave a small clap of her hands. Then, as if the idea just struck her, she added, "I'm going to get you a T-shirt and mug so we can get your picture for the website."

CHAPTER TEN

Lori waited at the inn for a full day, hoping Drake would take her up on her offer for dinner. She pretended to work on her travel article while sitting on the screened porch, but in reality she watched the road eagerly for travelers and flipped through the photos Sheriff Jackson hadn't deleted. Unfortunately, her wireless device hadn't picked up cellular service in the swamp and her images hadn't synced to back up to her cloud storage. She should have charged the device when she charged her camera, but she hadn't thought about it at the time since she was going to be going back to her hotel. When the sheriff deleted the pictures, he'd taken her only copies.

There was one depicting a very small image of Drake in his shifted form. It was his head peeking out of the water as she'd busily flashed her camera at the surrounding alligators. Well, honestly, it could be his head in the shadows surrounded by tree limbs, or just another alligator. She had one of his human self as he watched the paramedics take Big Daddy from the airboat.

That was all she had—a tiny maybe dot of his lizard man head and part of his human face.

The idea of the lizard man frightened her, but the memory of the man caused her to ache. Yes, much of it was sexual desire. She was undoubtedly attracted to him. But there was more. She found she wanted to look at him, study the scar, ask him questions about these Var and Draig. There were more shifters out there in the world. There had to be. This man had come from somewhere.

Then there was the man himself. He'd saved her. She sensed the goodness in him and was not afraid.

Maybe she was crazy. Maybe she'd imagined the photos and the sheriff's threats. She'd been scared when Drake had come on to the airboat. It had been dark. Alligators had her adrenaline pumping. She was creative and prone to imagining. Like the time she'd been convinced her house was haunted because of thumping in the walls. Twelve séances and a cleansing later, it had turned out to be old, loose pipes.

No, Drake was real. She remembered his kiss, his touch, his hesitance and his eagerness. If any other man had started talking about marriage after one day, she'd have run for the hills. But remembering Drake do it made her want to head to the bayou.

The photo of Drake by the paramedics was tagged with GPS data. Past experience told her it wouldn't be exact, but it would get her close to where he lived. The backroads the sheriff had taken were a winding maze, but she had to try. No part of her could accept that this was it. One morning and then nothing? She would spend the rest of her life wondering, her mind stuck forever on that one event, unable to move on.

"Are those the pictures from your adventure?" Mr. Howards's voice startled Lori, and she jolted up in her chair. She'd angled her body so that people couldn't see her screen from behind her…well, unless they crept up to purposefully gaze over her shoulder.

Automatically, she reached for her laptop and closed it to hide the pictures of Drake's maybe head in the water. "Just a few swamp landscapes."

Mr. Howards chuckled. "If I knew you better, I'd say something in those waters has you spooked."

"Yes. Hungry alligators." She reached to pull the power cord from the wall plug.

"Would you like to talk about it?" he asked. "You seem shaken up."

"Thanks for the offer, but I'm all right." She tapped her laptop a couple of times. "Just deadlines. Lots of deadlines."

Ah, the perfect excuse—even if it was true most of the time. No one ever asked for more details about deadlines.

"Take a break. Let me buy you dinner," he insisted.

"Oh," she said in surprise as she hurried to gather her laptop and camera bags. "That's very kind of you to offer, but I have to finish this article tonight. The news never sleeps."

Okay, so that one was a lie. She had a week before she had to turn it in.

"You won't regret it." Mr. Howards smiled. She could tell he was used to having his charming way, but there was something about his entitled personality that put her off.

"I would, but I'm meeting my fiancé—" she began.

"Janice told me you were single," he interrupted. "She thinks we'd be perfect for each other."

"Oh, well, Janice is a busybody who apparently can't be trusted with personal information." She hoisted her bags onto her shoulders. "I didn't inform her of my wedding plans."

"You're not wearing a ring," he pointed out.

"You don't take no very well," she stated. "Have a good evening, Mr. Howards."

CHAPTER ELEVEN

Drake felt a shiver of awareness course through his body. He jerked his head up from where he stared at the dark water. A car drove on the nearby dirt road. He stood next to the broken dock outside his home, listening for boats, as he did every night.

The emptiness building inside him since Lori had driven away with the sheriff was unbearable, the loneliness worse than ever before. How could humans not know when they had found their life mate? One look and he'd been sure. At the time, he hadn't realized what was happening on the airboat, but his body had known. He'd felt she was familiar to him.

He kept the sound of the car in the back of his thoughts as he concentrated on the water. Had the careless hunters taken to land, he could have tracked them. Since they stayed on a boat, he had to stand and wait for them to come back. Perhaps this was his purpose in life—standing on the shore waiting. Jackson had called him a guardian of the bayou.

Drake didn't want to be a guardian.

Duty demanded he do just that.

The ache filled him, radiating from the missing piece of his soul. He'd given it to Lori. With each passing hour, that much became clearer. One second was all it had taken. One look. One touch. One kiss.

One curse to live his days empty.

Guardian of the bayou.

Alone.

The gods were indeed cruel.

His shifted eyes peered over the water. In this form, he could better hear and see in the dark. He focused on the distant familiar details, watching for changes. The sound of the car slowed. It had come closer, but he ignored it. He again focused on the swamps.

Drake had no idea how long he stood in his misery, waiting. Suddenly, he frowned. Something was not right. He looked toward his home, then to the trees. The forest did not make its usual sounds. He directed his hearing toward the dirt road. No car. No motor. Footsteps. Animal? No. Two legs. Slow steps. Stop. Rustle of leaves.

Drake held perfectly still as he scanned the trees. The moon did not provide much light to help his search in the darker shadows. A tiny pop sounded, and he quickly turned his attention toward the noise. Fire erupted in his shoulder, forcing him to stumble backward.

"Nice shot! That's some fine hunting," someone yelled, the tone laughing and excited. "You got it, Mr. Howards."

Drake grabbed his shoulder and felt blood trickle over his fingers. The initial fire did not lessen. Pain burned its way down his arm and up his neck.

"Grab it," a quieter voice answered. "Don't let my trophy get away."

The sound of running footsteps crunched twigs and rocks. Drake stumbled again, a little dazed by what was happening. Another pop sounded. His leg hit the broken dock, and he fell back into the dark water. Liquid cocooned him as he bumped against the swamp bed. His leg jerked, but he couldn't move his arm to swim or defend himself. Another shot sounded, breaking the surface of the water. A light passed over him. He heard yelling but couldn't make out the distorted words.

Some guardian he'd turned out to be.

Another ache grew, worse than the pain in his body, as he thought about Lori. This was not how his journey was supposed to end.

CHAPTER TWELVE

"You're trespassing."

At least, that's what Lori thought the old woman said in thick Cajun English. Even if the words were translated incorrectly by Lori's brain, the fact Ursa held a rifle on her was easy enough to understand. She was trespassing, and she was not welcome.

This was Ursa? The woman who filled Drake's head full of nonsense and convinced him to drunken skinny dip in a fake Cajun induction ceremony? This was the woman Lori had been jealous of?

Ursa's thin, homemade dress hung on her small frame. But for all the look of frailty, Ursa held the gun steady. The woman had been easy enough to find once Lori had asked a couple locals...and bought a case of their local jams.

"My name is Lori," Lori stated loudly from her place on the woman's lawn. She was careful to keep her shaking arms lifted to her sides to show she wasn't a threat.

"I know who you are. Sheriff warned me about you," Ursa stated. Lori had to listen very carefully to understand her.

The small shack looked as if it had been built by hand a hundred years ago but had been maintained with loving care, or at least care out of necessity. Two flame lanterns and one battery-powered light illuminated the porch and yard. The owner, by all appearances, never left her piece of the swamp.

"Dat boy saved my life. He saves a lot of lives. Now you just get before dey…" The rest of the sentence was lost in a rapid, undecipherable stream of half Cajun English, half Cajun French threats that mumbled together only to be punctuated by the tilt of Ursa's gun.

"He saved me too. Were you trapped in the swamps?" Lori asked, trying to keep the conversation civil. At the moment, she couldn't picture Ursa needing help with anything. Her mind raced, hoping it wouldn't discharge. But it was hard to think of options when she couldn't quit staring at the end of the gun as metal glinted in the soft light.

"No. I know you know about Drake. De…" Again the words were lost.

"I'm sorry, I don't understand."

"I said no," Ursa repeated, talking slowly as if Lori was simpleminded. "I know you know about Drake. De sheriff told me. De night he arrived, coming out of dem swamps like a dragon-man creature from de bayou, I had a gun in my mouth. He saved me. God, gods, doesn't matter who sent him. He's here. He's my family. And in de backwaters, we have ways of protecting our family." Ursa lifted her rifle and pointed it steadily at Lori.

"People know to come looking for me here." Lori hoped the woman didn't detect the lie.

"Let dem come. Dem gators have dey usefulness."

Lori swallowed nervously and glanced over her shoulder to the distant water and then back to the gun. "Please. I just want to talk to him. If he tells me to leave him alone, I will."

"Shush!"

Lori jumped as Ursa charged forward. She scrambled to get out of the way. To her surprise, instead of threatening her further, the old woman went to the edge of the water and looked in. Lori didn't hear anything to warrant the apt attention. The croak of frogs punctuated the night, a singing backdrop over a fetid landscape.

With Ursa's attention turned away, the prudent thing would have been to run for her car. Lori's trembling limbs wouldn't move that fast, and instead she crept as quietly as she could toward freedom.

Michelle M. Pillow

"Stop moving. Sometin's out dere." Ursa lifted her gun and gestured it at the water, following a subtle ripple along the surface as it came closer.

Not knowing why she thought it, Lori whispered, "Drake."

Lori instantly changed course as she was drawn to the water's edge. She mindlessly placed her hand on the barrel to turn the weapon from the water. Ursa jerked the gun away from her.

"Don't," Lori said, watching the water. "Drake."

"How…?" Ursa lowered her gun.

"Drake?" Lori yelled, very sure that he was near.

At the sound of her voice, something broke the surface of the water. Drake looked just as he had when he'd come up from the swamp to rescue her, how he'd looked in the deleted pictures. Lori stiffened to see him in his shifted from. Somehow, seeing him was different now. She knew he was real.

She'd been calling him a lizard man, but he was more dinosaur than lizard. The light behind her shone on his face, contrasting the thick brown skin protruding over his nose. His lips were parted as he gasped for breath, showing the tips of his fangs. A taloned hand pressed to his shoulder as he came from the water.

His yellow eyes met hers and he stumbled.

"Drake?" Lori charged into the shallow water without thought. She caught him by his arm and steadied his steps. The hard shell of his body felt strange against her hand. Blood trickled over his fingers from his shoulder. She tried to hurry him out of the water and onto land. "What happened? Were you bit?"

His eyes met hers, eyes that were far from human, and yet she felt him in that gaze. The man was there, beneath the hard armor plating and scary visage. He had characteristics of a medieval dragon if that creature had mated with a human. "What are you doing here?"

His gruff voice sounded harsher than she remembered.

"I couldn't find you," Lori said. A rush of nerves and emotions built inside her. Everything she felt like saying sounded strange in her head. Following the impulse to jump into his arms and kiss him would be even stranger. Instead, she mumbled, "I found Ursa."

Ursa interrupted with a thick stream of accented words. Drake answered the woman in kind, fluently speaking to her as if he were a native to the bayou.

"What's going on?" Lori demanded, not understanding them.

"She offered to shoot you," Drake said.

Lori stiffened.

"I told her that is not necessary," he added.

90

Lori thought she saw him smile, but it was too hard to say.

Ursa grumbled and turned to her house. "Bring him."

"Why were you looking for me?" he asked when they were relatively alone.

"Why are you bleeding?" she demanded. "What happened?"

"It will heal." Drake leaned heavily on her even though she could tell he was trying not to.

"This isn't right. You need a doctor. My car is right over —"

"No doctors. I do not wish to be sent to Roswell. I have seen the pictures."

"The alien-conspiracy place? That's not real. It's a giant hoax. Aliens don't ex...ist." Lori suddenly realized how ridiculous that belief sounded given the circumstances.

"I assure you aliens are real. I have met several who have come to my planet."

"Alien," she whispered. That thought hadn't occurred to her. She'd slept with an alien. Not just a genetic offshoot of human, but an alien. Outer space. Alien. She breathed harder, trying not to hyperventilate. The weight against her arm grew, and if she left him now, he'd fall over.

"It amazes me how vain humans are to think they are the only lifeforms in the entire universes." He winced and pressed harder to his shoulder. She felt his muscle flex beneath her hand as they made slow progress to the porch.

"You need a hospital. Let me take you. I'll call the sheriff on the way and have him meet us. He seems protective of you. He'll run whatever interference you need." She tried to redirect his steps toward her car. "Can you shift back into your other self and look human again?"

"I will heal better in this form." He forced her to turn back toward the porch. "I need rest."

"Hurry up, boy," Ursa demanded from inside the home. "Guns are loaded. Dem assholes going to get a butt full of hot lead if dey try to cross my doorstep."

"Guns?" Lori repeated. "For the alligator that bit you?"

"For the hunters who shot me," he corrected.

"You're shot?" Lori gasped. Why wasn't he in a panic?

"It appears the people shooting at the shore were actually hunting aliens. It seems they thought I would make a trophy. Though, I'm not really an alien."

She glanced behind them toward the water before shoving him into a faster gait. He grunted in protest, but she didn't care. "What the hell? Dammit, Drake, get inside. How can you be so calm about this?"

"How is a shot worse than a bite?"

"Being hunted by humans is worse than being bit by an alligator in the swamp. An alligator isn't going to try and track you down to finish the—oh my God." Lori shook her head in denial. "He couldn't have… Oh my God."

"Are you praying for me?" Drake leaned against the door frame and stopped.

"It's my fault. Mr. Howards from the inn."

"I heard someone say that name," Drake said.

"He kept asking me about the lizard man. I told him nothing, but he seemed to think I knew where to find you. I thought my computer was glitching, but the inn has a public internet connection, and I think he must have hacked my machine and copied the photos I took outside your house. He could have used my GPS metadata to track you."

"I am not a lizard, and I am not technically an alien," Drake stated. "My people are dragon-shifters. It is said we lived here on Earth long ago and left through the portals to escape human persecution. Cat-shifters came with us. I have simply returned to the home of my ancestors"

"That is what you took away from what I said? You're worried about being mistaken for a lizard alien? Come on, we need to go inside. You can't go home." Lori made a small noise of exasperation and urged him to go inside the cabin. She shut the door. "Do you have a..." Lori's voice gave out as she looked around. Inside of Ursa's home wasn't some dirty backwater shack. Light came from a lamp on a highly polished table. The antique wood furniture complemented the pristine rugs and surrounded a giant flat screen television mounted on the wall over a fireplace. Shelves lined the side of the mantel, filled with DVDs.

"Don't get ideas," Ursa warned as if Lori was about to steal something.

"Drake needs medical attention," Lori said, not bothering to argue with the woman. "Why am I the only one who seems to get the urgency of this situation?"

"Why?" Ursa frowned. "He'll be fine. Always is." She jerked her thumb over her shoulder. "You know where to go, *chere*."

Drake nodded and moved to follow her direction to the dining room table. Ursa produced a sewing box from a cabinet and followed him. She opened the lid and took out a crude metal instrument and a bottle of whiskey. Handing him the drink, she then waited until

94

he took several gulps before beginning to probe at his shoulder.

Drake turned his attention to Lori. It was hard to see if he was in pain by the hardness of his shifted face. Lori approached him slowly.

"Why were you searching for me?" Drake asked. His eyes narrowed as Ursa poked around his wound.

"I..." Lori gave a small, helpless gesture. "You never came for dinner. I wanted to see you, to thank you, to, um, see you. How are you?"

Drake looked at his injured arm and back at her. "I am well."

Lori winced as Ursa shoved her instrument deeper into Drake's oozing shoulder. She remained quiet, watching the procedure with a feeling of horror.

Chapter Thirteen

What new test was this?

Sheriff Jackson had warned him away from Lori. Ursa wanted to shoot Lori. Both were people whose opinions he trusted. Drake wanted to keep Lori with him in the swamps as his mate, have babies with her and — if the gods ever blessed him with a way to make it happen — take her back to his home world to show her where he was born.

Drake stared at Lori, thinking of her to avoid feeling the pain in his arm. Ursa filled the silence, demanding the story of how Drake came to be on her lawn. He told her everything. There was no reason not to.

When Ursa finally dug the bullet from his arm, he was assaulted with an almost instant numbness as his body began to heal. The sound of metal clanked against porcelain when Ursa dropped the bullet into a container. She then dabbed at his arm.

"You don't look like a dragon," Lori said. "At least none that I've seen in mythology books."

"You are thinking of female dragon-shifters," he answered.

"I thought you said you came back to Earth because your people didn't have female dragons." Lori moved closer to him. He watched her expression for fear but didn't find any. Instead, she looked curious.

"Very few in our older generations," he answered. "But they are dying out. We have not had a female shifter birth on Qurilixen for a long time. When the problem first began, couples were encouraged to have more babies in hopes that it would result in some women. It did not work. All it did was make a large generation of men with little prospect of having a family."

"So you all decided to move back to Earth?" Lori asked.

"Our old documents say that humans are reproductively compatible. So the portal that was used to escape persecution on Earth was unburied. Unfortunately, no one can agree on how to go about finding brides. Some wish to cross over and take batches of them by force. Some want to move our populations over in segments and bring them back once they've mated. Some suggest we barter with your government. Though after living here, I think that is a mistake. I have seen how your people deal with outsiders. Some believe we are defying the will of the gods and wish to close the portal permanently so humans cannot come through. They think humans will taint shifter blood. But all this matters very little for the time being as the royal families have kept the portal from the population and are selfishly only letting royal members through to find wives."

Ursa snorted and gathered up her crude medical kit. "I'll call de sheriff and tell him about Howards."

Lori waited until the woman moved toward the kitchen before stepping closer to study Drake's arm. When they were alone, she asked, "Are you in pain?"

"Yes," he answered. It was the truth. His heart had ached since she'd left and now was filled with fear that she would go again. It was the most severe of pains.

"The royal families wish to control the population by blocking access to brides?" Lori inquired.

"I believe so." He remained in his seat, afraid if he moved he'd be tempted to hold her. If he held her, he'd want to kiss her. If he kissed her, he'd never let her go.

"Then how did you get to Earth?" Lori lightly touched his injured arm, keeping her fingers away from the wound.

"They will not let us make decisions for ourselves on whether we wish to come to Earth, but they let the new human princess come and go as she pleases. I waited, followed her and came through the portal after her." Drake remembered the fear he'd felt leaving his home. He'd often wondered if he'd made the right decision.

"Do you want to go back? You must be homesick."

"I miss parts of my home world. I miss the contrasting sweet and acrid smell of the mountain air. We only have darkness once a year. And there are three suns in the sky, not one. Many of our trees are as big as your redwoods, with smooth bubble-looking texture very unlike your rough bark that grows in shards. The leaves are much wider." He could recall the details so clearly, and yet he worried that one day the memory of home would fade. "The bayou reminds me of home, of the shadowed marshes near the borderlands where I grew up."

"Will you return? Or will they punish you for disobeying?" She stopped touching him and let her hand hang in the air between them.

"I doubt they've noticed I'm gone. If they do, I'm sure they'll suspect the Myrddin clan of doing me harm, but without proof or anyone to protest, they will not be forced to look into the matter. The friends I have said goodbye to will not betray me. I would like to return some day, but I am not sure I will ever find the way." Drake stared at her hand. She was so delicate and soft. Everything inside him wanted to protect her. How could he do that when he had people hunting him?

"If it's something you want, I'll help you. We can go to the French Quarter. You mentioned the LaLaurie Mansion. We can find —"

"It is a kind offer, but the portal does not open in the same place every night. I do not know when or if it will appear there again."

"Drake," Lori hesitated. Slowly, she reached for his shifted face. Her fingers moved over his hardened features. The protective shell of his armor dulled the sensitivity of his skin, but he still felt her. She traced his old scar.

"I must appear to be a monster to you," he said.

"The men who shot you are the monsters." Lori cupped his jaw and turned his face up to look at her. "You confuse me."

"I am not confused. I know what I feel." He traced the tip of a taloned finger down her arm.

"Does it hurt to shift?"

Drake chuckled. "No more than breathing."

"Can you do it whenever you want?"

"Yes."

"Will you show me?"

"No."

Lori stopped caressing him. "Is it because you'll die from the wound?"

"No."

"You don't want me to see?" She frowned.

"Being in dragon form tempers back my desires since I cannot make love to you in this body."

"Oh," she said, and then, as if realization hit her, she repeated louder, "Oh."

"If I were to shift, I might do something you don't want me to."

"What makes you think I don't want you to?" Her cheeks colored ever so slightly.

Drake stood from his chair to tower over her. His skin tingled as his body transformed into his human self. Her breath caught as she watched, but she did not pull away in fear. He leaned into her and pressed his lips to hers. The ache inside him instantly lessened at the contact.

Lori gasped and pulled away. "What was that?"

"Don't leave me again," he whispered.

"Ole Jack said to lock up and stay here," Ursa announced loudly. "Drake can hear sometin' coming ten miles away. I have guns, whiskey and cards." Ursa came from the kitchen holding all three items. "Everytin' for de *bourre*."

"Boo-ray?" Lori sounded out. She eyed the whiskey. "I don't know what that means, but it better not involve me having to strip down naked so you can make me a Cajun."

Ursa arched a brow and laughed. "No one is asking to see you naked. What fun is dere in dat for me?"

CHAPTER FOURTEEN

"Boo-ray" was some kind of card game. Lori didn't exactly know how to play it, but she was pretty sure Ursa kept changing the rules. She was also confident that Ursa moonlighted as a frat boy from a party house. The old woman might look frail, but she could knock back whiskey like the best of them and told loud, incomprehensible stories that couldn't have been appropriate by the way she cackled and winked after each one.

Whenever Ursa left the table to do her version of a perimeter check, Drake would sneakily drink Lori's whiskey for her. She'd nodded, grateful to him for recognizing she couldn't keep up with the two of them. Though she tried to tell Ursa she didn't want another drink, the woman kept trying to ply her with alcohol.

"Drake," Lori insisted when Ursa reached for a shotgun and made her way to the front window. "She shouldn't be carrying a loaded weapon."

Drake reached under the table to the chair next to him and then revealed a couple shotgun shells he'd hidden there. "She's not."

Lori gave a small laugh and relaxed. "How did you possibly become friends with Ursa?"

The woman hardly seemed like the ideal ambassador for first contact with an alien species…or a dragon-shifter former Earthling coming to his medieval ancestors' home.

"I found the swamps. She found me."

"I don't think it's that simple. She said you saved her life. That she was about to kill herself." Lori glanced over her shoulder. Ursa had stopped looking out the window and had taken up residence in a chair. The old woman stared at the wall, her eyes closing as she fought to stay awake.

Drake looked at Ursa and stood when the old woman didn't move. He held out his hand to Lori. "Come."

Lori followed him into a small room. He shut the door and turned on the light. Photographs lined the wall, filling nearly every conceivable space. An old quilt was neatly folded over a rocking chair. Tiny knickknacks and trinkets that would only make sense to their owner lined the dresser.

"All the pictures are of the same couple," Lori observed. The wall displayed the entire life of a couple, the photos arranged like the flow of memories in no particular timeline—a party, a cigarette, a dance, a laugh, a wrecked car, tears, a ruined pie, two forks in a piece of cake. They were the small moments that made a lifetime. As a photographer, she could appreciate the simplicity of the collection. As a woman, she felt envious of all that couple had and were. She pointed to a smiling woman in a 1950s wedding dress. "Is that Ursa?"

Drake nodded. "With her mate, Irving. Ursa lost her one true love. He died on their fiftieth anniversary. I arrived ten years after, on the anniversary of his death when she had decided to join him."

"I can't imagine," Lori whispered. She thought of the drunken woman holding an empty shotgun and suddenly felt very sorry for her tragic story. "To be with someone that long, to love them so much that time cannot heal you. I don't think anyone loves like that anymore. I mean, I've heard my grandparents' generation talking about love at first sight, marrying soldiers after one day before they head off to war. I can't rationalize doing something like that. Logically, it makes no sense to leap into major decisions."

Drake cupped her cheek. "Perhaps this is not something that needs your logic, but your heart. I watch you humans. You run haphazardly through life without stopping to breathe. You make decisions and then doubt them. You make new decisions and then doubt them as well. Sometimes, you don't make any decision and just let things happen regardless of consequences. I do not think life is so difficult. If you see a child in danger, you save it. If you see an animal in pain, you help it. If you are hungry, you find food. If you have responsibilities, you do your duty. And if you find love, you let yourself feel it. You grab on to it because that is the only thing that makes life worth living, and you never know when it will be taken away by the gods. If you find it, there is no need to look elsewhere. The Draig understand this. We do not divorce. We connect for life like Ursa did. When dragons mate, our lives extend to our partners, becoming so entwined that it is said humans live longer because of it. I think it is because we naturally want more time."

Lori saw the earnestness of his expression. She felt safe. Somewhere, out in the miles and miles of swamps and marshes was a maniac hunter with a gun, and yet she felt safe with Drake inside this little cabin in the middle of nowhere.

Her cheek tingled where he touched her. She swallowed, nervously, licking her lips. His gaze remained steady trained on hers. Tiny yellow swirls of color lined his pupils. Desire bubbled to the surface. It had been there all night, simmering and waiting. It wasn't only her body that tingled, but her mind. She felt a prickling in her brain like someone scratched to come inside her thoughts.

A combination of fear and anticipation filled her. She found herself moving closer to him until her body pressed against the length of his. He leaned his forehead to hers and did not look away. The physical needs of her body caused her mind to focus on the hard press of his shaft against her stomach. The heat of him warmed her clothing.

"What's happening?" she whispered. She couldn't move.

"Let me love you," he said. *"Let yourself love me."*

Lori pulled away. His lips hadn't moved when he said the last words, but she'd heard his voice inside her mind. "Wait, what did you say?"

"Let me love you." Again, his lips didn't move. *"I have to believe that my gods led me here, to you, for a reason."*

"Drake, stop that," she insisted before thinking, *"How are you in my head?"*

"We mated," he answered, this time using his mouth.

"Are you reading my thoughts? I mean, you know that…" Lori tried not to think of all the things she didn't want him to see—the memory of his naked body, the fantasies she'd had about that naked body, the desperate climax she'd experienced in the inn just thinking about him late at night, and imagining him all shifted and hard and fuck…

Drake grinned and let his eyes flash to gold and then back again. "The dragon skin is a protective armor, and I cannot take you in my shifted form, but if you want to be hunted like that I can—"

"Ah!" Lori hit his arm. "Let a girl have a little mystery to her."

"Why? You want me," he stated.

"Yes, I want you again, but—"

"Not just sex. You want to be my wife. You love me."

"No, no." She shook her head. *"That's absurd. It's been a couple of days. And stop smiling. And get out of my thoughts."*

"I like your thoughts," he directed back at her. He pulled her tightly against him. His skin rippled, and in the span of a few seconds, he stood before her in his

dragon form. She felt the shift along the length of her body, firm flesh turning to hard skin.

"Well, then I'm just going to have to…" Lori concentrated, trying to read his mind. At first, it was fuzzy and jumbled, but then she felt him. The sensation became a tickle of pure emotion, building until every feeling he had for her came flooding in. He'd told the truth. He'd loved her from the start. She felt the ache her leaving with the sheriff had caused. Never in her life had she imagined anyone missing her that much.

"Let me buy you flowers and cake." Drake let his body shift back into human form.

Lori laughed at the strange request. "Well, what girl doesn't like flowers and cake?"

"So yes?" Drake stroked her bottom lip with his thumb. "You accept that we are mated? Forever?"

"Marriage," Lori said in sudden understanding. Her laughter faded. Without hesitation, she answered, "Yes." She looked at the fifty years of a life filled with love on Ursa's wall. Her path suddenly became very clear. This is what she wanted. No more searching around the next corner. It didn't matter if she lived in a swamp if it meant she got to have a life filled with happiness. "Yes, Drake, I'll have flowers and cake with you."

CHAPTER FIFTEEN

Drake could not stop kissing his mate. Lori was everything he could have hoped for. The connection between them deepened with each passing second until he could feel her inside his soul. She was a vital part of him he could never live without.

Her aching need for him mirrored his need for her, and he fumbled to free her of her pants. Lori pulled at his waistband, freeing his arousal. In an eager joining of half-dressed bodies and desperate hands, they managed to come together against the door. He lifted her thigh, entering her without testing her depths. He didn't have to. He knew what she wanted.

The perfection of the moment was punctuated by harsh breaths and hushed sighs. They connected with more than flesh, and the deep bond would never be severed. Lori held on to him, gripping his shoulders as he lifted her other leg. The position allowed him deep, and he pumped himself into her. The tension built and he thrust harder and faster. Lori's release washed over him as she let him partake of her pleasure. The feelings were too much, and he orgasmed hard.

In the aftermath, he did not let her go. He held her close. "I pledge to do everything I can to make you happy, Lori."

"You already have, Dra—"

Her words were cut off by a loud crash coming from the front of the house. Drake instantly shoved her behind his back and faced the door. He'd been so focused on Lori and the connection between their bodies and souls that he hadn't been paying attention to potential dangers.

"Get out of my house!" Ursa yelled belligerently. There was a sound of a struggle.

Drake jerked up his pants and whispered. "Stay here."

"Guns don't work without bullets," a man mocked from the other room. "Give me that before you hurt yourself."

"Drake," Lori whispered and grabbed his arm, and he felt her fear.

"Stay," he insisted. When he'd taken Ursa's bullets, he'd thought he was protecting her. It was now his fault she was left helpless.

"All we want is the lizard man," a man said.

"That's Howards," Lori said. "He must have tracked you here."

"Where are you hiding it?" Mr. Howards yelled at Ursa.

Ursa responded with a string of confrontational words.

"We know it's hiding here. There are tracks coming from the swamp." The sound of slamming doors followed Mr. Howards's statement.

Drake slowly opened the door to assess what was happening. Ursa lay on the floor, trembling and holding her face. Still, despite her obvious pain, she continued to curse the two men and all of their descendants. Howards was a larger man and directed more than helped a second, smaller man to knock DVDs off the shelves.

Drake tried to move undetected to gain the advantage and keep the men from firing the guns around the women, but the door hinge creaked and gave his position away. Drake sprang into action, surging forward. He shifted as he attacked, using his taloned hand to swipe at the nearest opponent.

"Kill it, Mr. Howards, kill it!" the smaller human yelled in fright and flailed around, wielding his rifle as a club because Drake was too close to shoot. He struck

Drake's chest, but the metal barrel barely registered against the dragon-shifter armor.

Gunfire sounded behind Drake as Howards shot at his back. The bullet grazed his thigh and struck the rifle-club wielding man in the hip. The man screamed and fell back, dropping his weapon. He grabbed his injury and crawled across the floor to the open front door.

Chaos erupted. Drake saw Lori from the corner of his eye. She charged Howards. The hunter fired again, but the shot went wide as Lori flung her body against the man's arm. Ursa grabbed Mr. Howards's ankle and pulled. The hunter shouted in protest at the attack. He kicked and punched to get the women off him. Ursa and Lori both sustained blows but kept fighting. Mr. Howards angled the butt of his rifle toward Lori.

Drake roared. The sound reverberated off the cabin walls. He reached the man as the rifle swung down. His talons ripped into the hunter's arm, and he jerked the weapon out of his hands and threw it aside.

Unlike his terrified partner, Mr. Howards didn't stop fighting. He reached for his waist and pulled a handgun. He aimed it at Ursa's head as she held on to his leg. Drake reacted, tearing through the man's neck and shoulder with one slash of his hand. The gun never fired and dropped out of the man's hand. Mr. Howards grabbed his neck to stop the flow of blood, but the wound was too deep. He crumbled to the floor.

"Drake," Lori whispered, her voice small.

Drake turned to the door. He blocked the women with his body.

"Go," he ordered, worried that more hunters were coming for them. "Take Ursa and run. I'll fight them off."

"This is the police," Sheriff Jackson shouted from outside. "Ursa? Drake?"

Drake dropped his arms slightly in relief to hear his friend's voice.

"Come in," Ursa yelled from her place on the floor. "You're late to de party. Punch bowl is empty, and I'm going to bed."

Lori offered Ursa a hand and helped her to her feet. Drake didn't relax his guard until he saw the sheriff enter.

Jackson eyed the bloody mess on Ursa's floor. "Ah, hell, Ursa, what did you go and do? I told you to lock the door."

"They broke in," Lori said, using Drake's arm for support as she inched past the dead body. "It was self-defense. I'll testify to it. This is Mr. Howards. He's a big-game hunter staying at Planation Inn. He hacked my computer and found where Drake was and tried to hunt him. He's a sick bastard. And they shot Drake." She motioned at his healing shoulder and then his leg. "Twice."

Ursa waved a dismissing hand at Lori and pointed to Mr. Howards. "Dat one shot de other one who bled out on de porch and I, um—" she tilted her head and studied the giant gash on Mr. Howards's body, "—bit dis one in de neck and he bled out right here. I was all by myself, minding my own, when dey came in and start wrecking de place. Left me no choice. I'm just a little old lady, all alone in de swamp, so helpless and—"

"All right, all right," the sheriff interrupted. Ursa chuckled to herself, the sound more of a cackle.

"I killed them," Drake stated. "I will accept my punishment."

"You weren't even here," Ursa denied. "You're not here now."

The sheriff looked at Mr. Howards. "I think you're confused Ursa. You must have stabbed him with a kitchen knife. Must have been cooking when they surprised you."

"Dat is it," Ursa said. She limped over to where the hunter's gun had fallen to the floor and picked it up. She moved toward her bedroom. "Dis is mine now. I'm going to bed. Lock up when you're done dragging out de..."

"Uh, Ursa, that's evidence. I have to take it with me." The sheriff followed her.

"No, you don't," Ursa yelled. "Dis is a nice gun. Take my old —"

***

Lori couldn't stand in Ursa's living room any longer. The cabin felt too small, and the smell of blood was making her sick to her stomach. She rushed to the front door. Mr. Howards associate was dead on the porch, having been shot in an artery if the blood pool was any indication. She hurried past the body and instantly began walking toward her car.

"Lori, wait." Drake chased after her.

Trembling, she turned to face him. "I am so sorry, Drake. This is my fault."

He stopped walking. "You are apologizing to me? It was my duty to protect you. I should have heard them coming."

"I should have known that he would track you here," Lori said. "You were so calm, and I thought it would be safe. If he hacked my computer to find you, he probably also put a tracker on my car. This could be my fault."

"You cannot control the evil in other men," Drake stated. "The gods have seen to it that he has been punished. Perhaps that was their will. They wished for us to end Mr. Howards's murdering ways."

His answer was so simple, so pure, and she could tell he believed it. "I don't know if I said it out loud, but I love you."

"I know. I feel it in you." He inched closer. "And you feel it in me."

"If I'm going to stay here with you, if we are going to make this work, we're going to have to talk about these alligator swims of yours, and about getting Internet service at your house so I can work. Do you even have a job? And no more hunters. I can't handle being shot at. And—"

Drake grimaced and held his temple.

"What is it? Are you injured?" She closed the distance to him and reached for his face.

"Do all female brains spin with thoughts and worry as yours does?" He gave her a wary look. "It was very scary in your brain just now."

"Well," she answered, wrapping her arms around his neck, "at least now I know how to get you out of my thoughts."

Epilogue

"Uh, Drake?"

Drake felt his wife calling to him in his mind as he swam beneath the water. Something hadn't been quite right about the ambient noise of the swamp, and he wanted to make sure his pregnant wife was safe. The full force of her apprehension filled him, and he quickened his pace.

"Drake, you have company." He saw a flash of reptilian eyes in his mind as he heard her words.

Drake surged up from the water and leaped onto the shore. His worried gaze found Lori standing on the porch, not daring to move. Lori pointed to the tree line near the water to a gathering of yellow reptilian eyes staring back at her in the evening light. She'd seen him shifted on many occasions, but that apparently hadn't prepared her for a yard full of dragons looking as if they'd just arrived from a refugee camp. Half a dozen men turned to look at him.

"Dimosthenis, thank the gods we have found you," Galen said, relaxing his stance. He stood in shifted form, speaking their native Draig language. He was a guard at the royal palace, and by all memories, a very loyal dragon to the ruling family. "We feared you were lost in the city of plague, but then we found this—" the man held up a brochure for swamp tours, "—and knew this was where you would be waiting for us if you made it out alive."

"Galen?" Drake couldn't believe what he was seeing. Since he had been swimming naked, Drake grabbed a pair of shorts off the edge of the broken dock and slid them on. Though he didn't know all the men now facing him, Drake recognized a few of them as workers from the palace. "I don't understand. How did you find me?"

"See." Galen offered the worn, crumpled brochure forward. "The shadowed marshes. The gods pointed us to you. It is their will. We were able to determine when you made it through. Then we waited for the right time so that we could track you."

"Are you here to take me back?" Drake edged closer to his wife. He'd fight them all if he had to. "I will not go easily."

"Drake?" Lori asked in his mind. He held up his hand to her in an effort to calm her fears.

"We're here to follow you," Galen said. Those behind him nodded eagerly in agreement. "You had the courage to leave, to forge a path into the unknown." The man looked at Lori and began to breathe hard as if emotions welled inside him. "To find a wife. All the things the royals seek to deny us and keep for themselves. One Var prince and one Draig prince have wives. The other two refuse to choose and yet journey here whenever they wish. They deny the rest of us a chance at happiness. You are a legend, and we would like to be like you, Dimosthenis. Please, do not send us away. We cannot go back to the city of plague. The trials those humans face are most horrible."

"Retching in the streets," someone added behind Galen. The dragon-shifter stepped forward to make himself seen. "Whipped into a frenzy of dancing and screaming. And they laugh as they spill their pickled insides onto the streets."

"We have faced that challenge and have proven ourselves," Galen said, touching the man's arm in a comforting gesture. He then turned back to Drake. "Help us to understand this world."

"Drake?" Lori asked out loud. She couldn't understand his native language. The dragon-shifters turned to face her in unison.

Drake let his body shift into human form. Using the Earth language, he said, "May I introduce to you my wife, Lori."

"Wife," the men repeated as if awed by the very word. They too shifted into their human forms as they eyed Lori intently.

"Then it is true. Earth has women for us." Gerard pushed his way forward. He'd worked taking care of ceffyls in the royal stables and normally kept to himself. Since he'd worked in the palace, his English was much clearer. "Lady Lori, you will show us how to capture women and make them our mates? You will show us which villages to raid, so we do not get plague carriers?"

Lori opened her mouth and made a weak noise before saying, "Uh, well, I think you're thinking of the medieval period, and I, uh, well—"

"I am an honorable man," another dragon-shifter interrupted enthusiastically. His English was thickly accented, much like Drake imagined he'd sounded when he'd first arrived. "When the portal again opens, I am to meet my brothers. There are seven of us. I would like to find a woman who will give me many children. And my brothers will need wives as well. We will live together in the forest as we did on Qurilixen. You will find me a woman who is not like those in the giant board drawings?"

"Giant...?" Lori looked helplessly at Drake. The men edged closer to her.

"Models," Drake supplied. "I believe he means billboards. He doesn't want a..." Drake paused and drew his hands up and down in front of him in a straight line. "He wishes for a woman with..." Drake gestured as if to draw voluptuously curved hips in the air.

"Oh," Lori said in surprise as she got his meaning.

"I am trained in combat. You can find me one to protect? I would bring a woman to my home and lock her there where she is safe," Galen said. "The royals have said how fragile human women are. That is why they do not want us coming here to get them. But I promise I will not let her out of the home so she cannot be injured."

"Oh, all right," Lori said in an authoritative tone. She lifted her hands with a decisive air to stop them from talking. "First, welcome to Earth. I'm sorry you had to enter through the French Quarter—"

"City of plague," Drake supplied.

"Which is not a city of plague," Lori continued. "It is a place of celebration where college kids go to party and woman take off their shirts in exchange for, you know what, never mind. As far as you're concerned, it's a city of plague. Stay away from it. We'll find you a nice church picnic or something to try first. In fact, you might want to stay out of most towns until you get a little more acclimated to the planet. Baby steps."

"I would like babies," the man with seven brothers inserted.

"As would I," another added.

"And I," said another.

"I would be happy just to have a woman," Galan said. "And babies if she is not too delicate to be filled with the dragon seed."

"Ok, ground rules time," Lori said, touching her rounded stomach. "No one says the words dragon and seed together in a sentence."

"As you wish, my lady," Galen said. "So you will help us?"

Lori looked at Drake. He couldn't help the happiness he felt when he looked at her. Telepathically, he said, *They have nowhere else to go, chere. Look at them.*

Slowly, Lori turned at the request to eye the tattered gathering of dragon-shifters before her. They had clearly been traveling for a long time and were tired. "You can stay here for now until we figure something out. We can't have you running about the countryside like a swarm of bayou lizard men. The last thing we need is Janice at the Plantation Inn to get wind of your existence."

"I will make this Janice a fine husband," one of them said. "Janice is a woman?"

"First things first. Come inside. Eat. Sleep. And tomorrow we will discuss—"

"Plans for the village raid?" Galen inserted eagerly.

"Earth etiquette," Lori corrected.

"And I will speak to Ursa about making you all Cajun," Drake stated. "I hope she has enough moonshine to perform this many ceremonies."

"Oh, I'm sure she'll figure it out," Lori said, chuckling. She waved the men into their home. "Find a place to rest. Try not to break anything."

Drake met his wife on the porch and pulled her into his arms. "They heard tales of my coming through the portal and followed. I do not wish to turn them away. They didn't even think to hide their dragons from you. I cannot let them roam around like that. And I cannot send them home after they defied royal orders not to come to Earth."

Lori slid her hands up his chest to rest them on his shoulders. "Drake, I would never ask you to send your friends away. They need us. And Earth women clearly need us to protect them from some very well-meaning but terribly misguided Romeos."

"They are dragons, not Romeos," Drake said, confused.

"My mistake," she answered, leaning up on her toes to offer her mouth for a kiss. It was an offer he gladly accepted.

"Lady Lori," Galen called, "we found this box with women in it. You will take us to find them?"

"Box...?" Lori gasped. "My photos. They're in my office. I had those proofs organized for the book, oh my God, stop!" She rushed into the house.

Drake smiled as he stood alone on the porch and listened to the chaos inside. This was how life was supposed to be—filled with love, purpose, and family.

The End

The series Continues

Captured by a Dragon-Shifter

Determined Prince

Rebellious Prince

Mischievous Prince

Headstrong Prince

Stranded with a Cajun

More to Come!

MichellePillow.com

NATIONAL BESTSELLING AUTHOR
MICHELLE M. PILLOW

Michelle M. Pillow, *Author of All Things Romance*™, is a multi-published, award winning author writing in many romance fiction genres including futuristic, paranormal, historical, contemporary, fantasy and dark paranormal. Ever since she can remember, Michelle has had a strange fascination with anything supernatural and sci-fi. After discovering historical romance novels, it was only natural that the supernatural and love/romance elements should someday meet in her wonderland of a brain. She's glad they did for their children have been pouring onto the computer screen ever since.

Michelle loves to travel and try new things, whether it's a paranormal investigation of an old Vaudeville Theatre or climbing Mayan temples in Belize. She's addicted to movies and used to drive her mother crazy while quoting random scenes with her brother. Though it has yet to happen, her dream is to be in a horror movie as 1. A zombie or 2. The expendable screaming chick who gets it in the beginning credits. But for the most part she can be found writing in her office with a cup of coffee in pajama pants.

She has been on the Amazon bestseller list multiple times, nominated for the Romantic Times Lifetime Achievement Award 2011, the winner of the 2006 RT Reviewers' Choice Award, nominated for the 2007 RT Award, a Brava Novella Contest Finalist and a PAN member of RWA.

Michelle has titles published with The Raven Books, Pocket Books, Random House, Virgin Books, Adam's Media, Samhain Publishing, Running Press, and more.

She loves to hear from readers. They can contact her through her website www.michellepillow.com

Michelle M. Pillow, Online

Michelle loves hearing from readers and can be found interacting on social media.

Author Website: http://www.MichellePillow.com

Pillow Talk Blog:
http://www.michellepillow.com/blog

The Raven Books:
www.TheRavenBooks.com

Facebook:
https://www.facebook.com/AuthorMichellePillow

Twitter: @MichellePillow

Book Release Newsletter:
http://michellepillow.com/newslettersignup/

DRAGON LORDS BOOKS

Related to Captured by a Dragon-Shifter Series

Dragon Lords Series

Barbarian Prince

Perfect Prince

Dark Prince

Warrior Prince

His Highness The Duke

The Stubborn Lord

The Reluctant Lord

The Impatient Lord

The Dragon's Queen

Lords of the Var Series

Part of the Dragon Lords World

The Savage King

The Playful Prince

The Bound Prince

The Rogue Prince

The Pirate Prince

More Coming Soon!

JOIN THE CLUB!

www.facebook.com/groups/MichellePillowFanClub

COMPLIMENTARY MATERIAL

The following material is free of charge. It will never affect the price of your book.

Warlocks MacGregor: Love Potions

Contemporary Paranormal Magickal Scottish Warlocks

A little magickal mischief never hurt anyone…

Erik MacGregor, from a clan of ancient Scottish warlocks, isn't looking for love. After centuries, it's not even a consideration…until he moves in next door to Lydia Barratt. It's clear that the shy beauty wants nothing to do with him, but he's drawn to her nonetheless and determined to win her over.

Lydia Barratt just wants to be left alone to grow flowers and make lotions in her old Victorian house. The last thing she needs is a demanding Scottish man meddling in her private life. Just because he's gorgeous and totally rocks a kilt doesn't mean she's going to fall for his seductive manner.

But Erik won't give up and just as Lydia let's her guard down, his sister decides to get involved. Her little love potion prank goes terribly wrong, making Lydia the target of his sudden embarrassingly obsessive behavior. They'll have to find a way to pull Erik out of the spell fast when it becomes clear that Lydia has more than a lovesick warlock to worry about. Evil lurks within the shadows and it plans to use Lydia, alive or dead, to take out Erik and his clan for good.

EXCERPT

"Ly-di-ah! I sit beneath your window, laaaass, singing 'cause I loooove your a — "

"For the love of St. Francis of Assisi, someone call a vet. There is an injured animal screaming in pain outside," Charlotte interrupted the flow of music in ill-humor.

Lydia lifted her forehead from the kitchen table. Her windows and doors were all locked, and yet Erik's endlessly verbose singing penetrated the barrier of glass and wood with ease.

Charlotte held her head and blinked heavily. Her red-rimmed eyes were filled with the all too poignant look of a hangover. She took a seat at the table and laid her head down. Her moan sounded something like, "I'm never moving again."

"You need fluids," Lydia prescribed, getting up to pour unsweetened herbal tea from the pitcher in the fridge. She'd mixed it especially for her friend. It was Gramma Annabelle's hangover recipe of willow bark, peppermint, carrot, and ginger. The old lady always had a fresh supply of it in the house while she was alive. Apparently, being a natural witch also meant in partaking in natural liquors. Annabelle had kept a steady supply of moonshine stashed in the basement. If the concert didn't stop soon she might try to find an old bottle.

"*Ly-di-ah!*"

"Omigod. Kill me," Charlotte moaned. "No. Kill him. Then kill me."

"*Ly-di-ah!*"

Erik had been singing for over an hour. At first, he'd tried to come inside. She'd not invited him and the barrier spell sent him sprawling back into the yard. He didn't seem to mind as he found a seat on some landscaping timbers and began his serenade. The last time she'd asked him to be quiet, he'd gotten louder and overly enthusiastic. In fact, she'd been too scared to pull back the curtains for a clearer look, but she was pretty sure he'd been dancing on her lawn, shaking his kilt.

"Omigod," Charlotte muttered, pushing up and angrily going to a window. Then grimacing, she said, "Is he wearing a tux jacket with his kilt?"

"Don't let him see you," Lydia cried out in a panic. It was too late. The song began with renewed force.

"He's..." Charlotte frowned. "I think it's dancing."

Since the damage was done, Lydia joined Charlotte at the window. Erik grinned. He lifted his arms to the side and kicked his legs, bouncing around the yard like a kid on too much sugar. "Maybe it's a traditional Scottish dance?"

Both women tilted their heads in unison as his kilt kicked up to show his perfectly formed ass.

"He's not wearing…" Charlotte began.

"I know. He doesn't," Lydia answered. Damn, the man had a fine body. Too bad Malina's trick had turned him insane.

To find out more about Michelle's books visit
www.MichellePillow.com

71628418R00083

Made in the USA
Lexington, KY
22 November 2017